PRAISE F

PEARRY TEO'S

BEDLAM STORIES

THE BATTLE FOR OZ AND WONDERLAND
BEGINS

Christine Converse

Bedlam Stories LLC
A Division of Teo Ward Productions
Los Angeles, CA

ISBN: 1492116564
ISBN-13: 978-1492116561

ACKNOWLEDGMENTS

S pecial thanks to Chad Michael Ward (as always) for his passion and dedication to his art that makes the style of Bedlam Stories possible. Nicole Jones, P. Emerson Williams and James Curcio for being there for us from day one. And especially to Marsha Eisenberg for all your hard work in taking this to new depths of hell. So big a lore with so many details that this franchise would not be possible without the dedication, passion and emotional support.

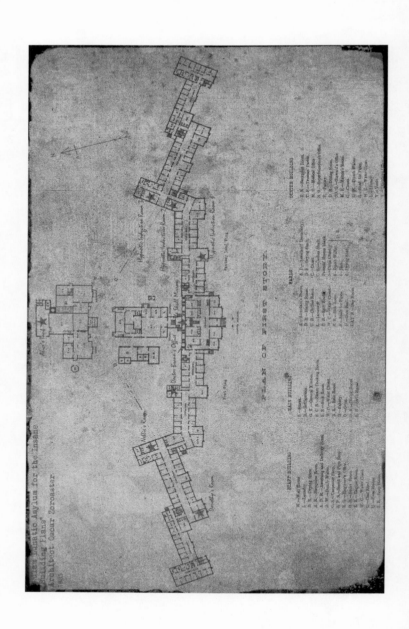

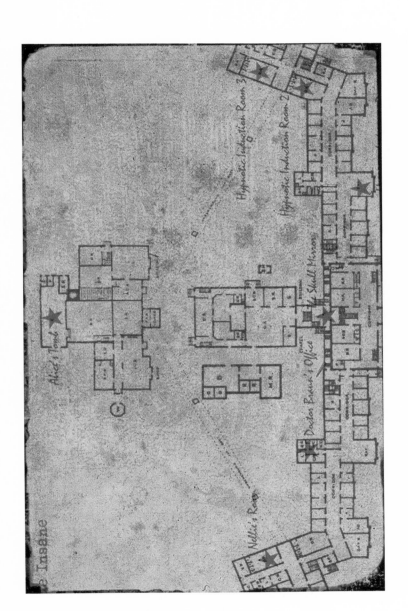

Insane

Alice's Pond

Nellie's Room

Doctor Bruner's Office

The Skull Mirrors

Hypnotic Induction Room 3

Hypnotic Induction Room 2

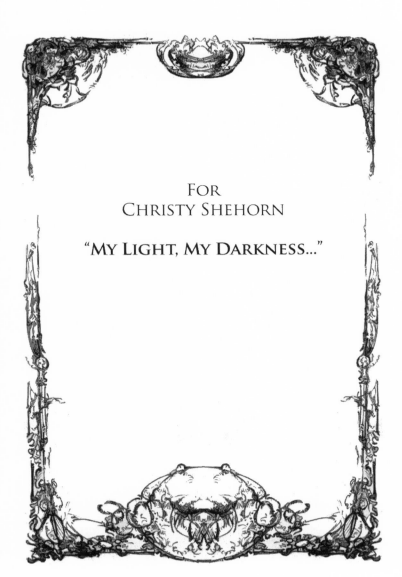

For
Christy Shehorn

"My Light, My Darkness…"

FOREWORD

I first met Pearry Teo years ago at one of my concerts in Phoenix, Arizona. I was on stage singing when I suddenly noticed there was a big screen next to the stage and while I was performing, they were playing a film. To be honest, my first reaction was one of mild annoyance. I thought, why would they play a film during a live performance? I feared people might decide to watch the film instead of me! And then a strange thing happened. I found *myself* watching that damn film!

On that screen, I saw a beautiful Asian woman surrounded by what looked like an undulating burst of black petrol, tendrils swirling and reaching out in different directions. I thought that it looked an awful lot like the living "Biologic" suit that my main character, Chi-chian wears in my first comic book of the same name. Then I realized that the actress on the screen was Bai Ling, who incidentally had voiced the character of Chi-chian when SyFy channel had hired me to make an animated webseries for their website. I thought to myself, wait a minute, did someone go and make a Chi-chian live action film without telling me? I'm pretty sure I forgot the lyrics of whatever song I was supposed to be singing at that moment.

It turns out that the film was Gene Generation by Pearry Teo and that the comic book company that published his comic books (on which the film is based) rented a booth at my show to promote the film.

When you experience something like that as an artist, I think it's a very common knee-jerk reaction to think someone ripped you off. But as time goes by (and as it happens again and again) I think more and more that incidents like these are more accurately explained as 'great minds thinking alike." Now I'm not referring to cases where someone sees your work and is directly inspired by it to create something similar (although that's wonderful!). I am talking about two or more people, growing up in the same world, at the same time, with similar interests, being bombarded by the same cultural stimuli, then being lead by these forces to reach a similar conclusion and create works that are very much alike to each other.

As a child, drawing monsters on countless pads of paper and later making stop-motion films in my basement, I felt like the world was filled with all manner of amazing, original concepts; monsters and creatures, chimeras, flights of fancy and unbridled fantasies. It seemed to me as a child, like the human imagination was highly unique to the individual and completely limitless. I certainly thought mine was.

But as of a decade or two ago, I began to have a nagging feeling that everything I saw seemed all too clearly inspired by something else or was filled with references to a dozen concepts that came before. Worse than that, no matter how original a concept I thought I had personally come up with, I would eventually see it pop up somewhere else.

When the film, Suckerpunk came out, I think I gasped out loud in the movie theater several times and quite possibly even cried at one point. Not only were there a dozen moments that seemed right out of the pages of my Chi-chian comic book, but they had even cast Emily Browning, who was my dream actress for a live action Chi-chian film that was proposed at the time (And naturally, there was a good deal of jealously involved that it was they and not me who were able to bring these visions to the big screen!).

In the early nineties, I wrote (but never quite finished or published) a novel called The Nothing. In essence, it explores issues of our existence on Earth and the nature of reality. It asks questions like what is God? Is there a God? How does the universe work, etc.

Recently, while considering finishing it, I Googled "The Nothing" to see what else was out there and found there had been a film made in 2012 by a director named Joshua Childs. The film is described as exploring the answers to the questions, "Is there a God? If so, does he care about us? Does anything truly matter?" Wait! What? REALLY?

What was happening? I certainly wasn't delusional enough to think that all of these artists and filmmakers had somehow found my incredibly obscure, Chi-chian comic book or the unpublished scribbles that exist of The Nothing and copied them! No. That would require some seriously deranged thinking. It was then that I began to believe in something like Carl Jung's collective unconscious... where we as humans inherently think similarly, organizing the information around us into similar conclusions, or... perhaps something even bigger is at work, where all of the thoughts of humankind are actually linked in some way and our collective mind leads a great many of us to create the work that is demanded by the events leading up to the present.

As an artist, this lead me to a good deal of despair as I pondered the following question; had we reached a point in human history where nothing new could be created?

It's no hyperbole when I say that this notion caused me a good deal of discomfort and nearly stymied my ability to create for a while. But eventually, I came to console myself with this rationale; perhaps, all of the ingredients for making art are already in existence. And it is not the creation of these ingredients but rather how they are assembled that leads us to a work of art being "original."

The concept of the villain, the hero, the love interest, the comedic side-kick, the fat, mentally ill guy in barbed wire wearing a pig head as a mask (okay, maybe not that last guy so much), these archetypes have existed for centuries. One or more of them appear in practically every story-driven work in existence. And yet, there are hundreds of combinations of these elements creating countless unique works.

Dozens of plot lines that we've seen rehashed and reworked in millions of TV shows, plays and novels have been in used for hundreds or thousands of years and yet when we get to the end of The Sixth Sense, we still gasp at the revelation it holds.

So perhaps, creating an original work is not about creating the building blocks themselves but about organizing a *combination* of these established elements in an original way. It's not unlike... cooking! All of the ingredients already exist... but there are endless recipes in existence and yet to be concocted.

As it happens, Pearry Teo is one hell of a cook!

I've followed his career as a filmmaker from the Sci-fi noir of his first film, Gene Generation, through the twisted, visceral horror of Necromentia and forward to become a director who knows how to inject his singular vision onto the screen.

Now, with Bedlam Stories, he's taken it to a whole new level! He's not merely assembled a tale using the building blocks of story and elements from our collective unconscious, he's ripped characters from our *universal consciousness*, namely the stars of Alice and Wonderland and The Wizard of Oz, and mashed them together in a horror epic that will have you reeling. Other artists have put a dark spin on these tales in the past, but never before have I seen someone take these two worlds, drag them into an insane asylum and create a whole new dark and delicious recipe from these beloved ingredients. When I read his Bedlam Stories screenplay a year or two ago, I was completely bowled over at the brilliance of this sinister combination, but now with the wonderful prose of author, Christine Converse, Pearry's world is richer than ever before. The horrors are darker and more unendurable and the blood is more vibrant on the asylum walls.

I no longer fear that nothing new can be created when here in my hands are familiar names and familiar faces and yet they have been transformed into something I could never have imagined. So crawl into bed, turn down the lights and prepare to be told the most nightmare-inspiring bed-time story you may ever hear.

Aurelio Voltaire
Musician, author, filmmaker
www.voltaire.net

PROLOGUE

Lifeless bodies littered the asylum floor. Papers fluttered through the air on currents of heat whipped to a frenzy by the chaos that filled the nearby hallways. These sheets that once held the prescription for sanity and the hope for a life outside these walls now fell, without reason, to die on the tiled floor, the last breath in this place now replete with death. Small fires provided scant light to penetrate the darkness that threatened to overtake her completely.

She used her good hand and all of her remaining strength to pull her bruised and battered body slowly across the floor toward the once white coat of a recently former orderly of the madhouse. Every inch forward wracked her body with pain, but it had been sheer will that had brought her through this nightmare, and it would continue to push her through what was to come next.

Her hand shook as she guided it into the pocket of the orderly's coat and found the thing she sought: a pen. The ringing in her ears continued as she pulled herself upward into a sitting position to rest against the wall. Her hand trembled, sliding one of the dirty pages from the floor to her side. Through the terror and exhaustion, she put pen to paper:

It seems strange that through some miracle I find myself alive, and the first thing I do is to find a piece of paper and write. I am, after all, a reporter at heart.

The worlds the girls have called Oz and Wonderland clashed together on this day.

She took a shuddering breath, closing her eyes for a moment to steel herself. She opened them again and forced a glance past the war zone to the horror at the asylum entrance: a carrion pile of bodies. Nurses, patients, orderlies, staff — they were hung, stapled and held together by iron chains, their dried blood serving as the mortar that sealed the grisly "bricks" to one another.

They were not fantasy lands or figments of youthful imagination. They were real — and inhabited by demons.

She now glanced in the opposite direction to the one item which, for its splendor and simplicity, had no place in this chamber of horrors. It alone remained pristine. On the wall, this ornate looking glass hung, reflecting its beauty the image of horror that compelled the woman to put pen to page.

This war began even before Dorothy and Alice met. And was I lucky or cursed that I was there to witness it all?

Pulling her hand to the top of the page, she marked the beginning of the account with the date.

October 23, 1922

CHAPTER 1

P ositively demented," murmured Dr. Raymond. He leaned back in his seat and stroked his beard. "I consider it a hopeless case. She needs to be put where someone will take good care of her."

Dr. Ward slowly nodded, following the movements of the shaking young woman before them. Her wispy black hair stood out from her thin pale face as if by electric shock. Her large brown eyes rolled from right to left and left to right, stopping only for a few moments to disappear completely behind fluttering eyelids and reveal the ghastly red-veins and yellowish-white eyeballs of a soul who had not slept in days.

Only Dr. Carandini remained unfazed, standing motionless in the shadows, arms folded, silently observing the woman hugging her knees to her chest and rocking to and fro.

"I do not concur."

Both men looked up, suddenly, to their compatriot. Dr. Raymond snatched his wire rim glasses from his face, quickly polished them on his lab coat, and returned them to his squinting eyes as if hoping to perceive some deeper truth about the girl sitting before them. Despite his efforts to gain clarity, the picture remained the same: Dr. Carandini remaining motionless, peering down his long nose to the quivering young woman.

"But she exhibits all the signs, sir!" Dr. Raymond exclaimed.

"Indeed," Dr. Carandini replied coolly, "A little too perfectly, would you not say?"

THUMP!

All three doctors turned back to the girl whose feet had slammed to the worn wooden floor. She gripped the creaking chair edges with such force that her fingertips turned red and her knuckles white. She leaned forward gradually — staring, bug-eyed, directly at Dr. Carandini, her pale, slender legs tensed against the chair.

The corner of Dr. Carandini's thin, hard mouth curled into a smirk.

"But doctor, with respect, sir, we have seen the tremors, the wild eyes...even the boarding house reports that she could not remember her whereabouts or how she arrived at their doorstep."

Dr. Carandini broke from the woman's gaze and turned his back to her. "Gentlemen, if you wish to sign your names to a false committal into Dr. Braun's brand of quackery, have at. I, for one, shall not be party to it because this girl is clearly playing you both for fools."

"Only a vampire would stay in the shadows," the woman murmured, her head tilting awkwardly to one side. "Needs to have his head cut off … cut off … cut-cut-cut-cut off-off-off-off-off …." The whispered words trailed off until they morphed into off-key humming.

Dr. Ward's chair slid backward an inch, away from

the woman, while Dr. Raymond scribbled on his clipboard. The woman jerked her head to stare at Dr. Ward, her pallid face abruptly breaking into a maniacal grin. His chair slid back another inch when she tilted her head, a long silvery strand of saliva rolling out of the corner of her mouth and stretching to the floor.

"Yes dear. And my palms are covered in hair, and my ears are pointed," Dr. Carandini said, dismissing her with a wave of his hand. "Can you please quit this charade, girl, so we can attend to the truly needy?"

The woman, whose gaze had, since the word "pointed" been fixed upon Dr. Carandini's right ear, did not respond.

"Miss ... erm ... Bly, was it?" Dr. Ward snatched the clipboard and fountain pen from Dr. Raymond and scribbled his signature across the admittance papers. "I am certain you will benefit from Dr. Braun's therapies. You have my approval." He briskly stood, tugged his lab coat into place, and with a click of heels and a nod to his contemporaries, promptly exited without a backward glance.

Dr. Raymond added his signature to the second line of physician recommendations and pushed the wire rim glasses up the bridge of his nose. He held the clipboard out to the nurse standing quietly behind the woman's chair.

"There you are, Miss Pretorious. The matter now rests with Dr. Carandini. Should he decline to concur, please file the papers with the court for the review of Judge Ostrow." He stood and glanced nervously toward the woman, following her still unbroken gaze to Dr. Carandini's head.

"Yes, sir," the nurse nodded, taking the clipboard. "Shall I call for the orderlies?"

"Cut-cut-cut-cut ... " the woman whispered.

Dr. Raymond pulled a handkerchief from his pocket and dabbed lightly at his forehead. "Yes, I think that would be best."

Dr. Carandini pulled his pocket watch from his waistcoat and flipped it open.

"Shall we to tea, then, Chadswor —"

The seemingly frail woman in the tattered dress

lunged from her chair and sprang, with doglike frenzy and a banshee screech, at Dr. Carandini, her outstretched fingers talons that locked, deathly tight, around his throat. He did not have time to react before flailing backward across a table filled with glasses, which collapsed under the force and weight of the assault, the glass shattering beneath them as they crashed to the floor.

Dr. Carandini's yelp of surprise precipitously became a howl of pain as the woman sank her teeth into his right earlobe, clenching her jaw with all the strength she could muster.

"EZEKIEL! FRANK!" the nurse threw open the door to scream down the hall. The sound of running feet, breaking furniture, and crunching glass could barely be discerned over the doctor's howls as the two tussled, rolling between scattered chairs and the overturned table.

Orderlies in white coats and thick, black, rubber-soled shoes sprinted to the rolling pair and pulled at any body part upon which they could gain purchase, but the woman clung tenaciously to Dr. Carandini with an iron grip. Frank dug his fingertips deeply into the meat of the woman's right bicep, sending shooting pain up her arm and causing her to involuntarily loosen her grip. He used the opportunity to yank the woman upward, away from the doctor, affording him a view of the blood flowing from the ragged flesh that now dangled from the doctor's ear. Still, the woman clung to the doctor with her free hand, kicking and scrabbling, growling incessantly.

Dr. Carandini clutched at a vase rolling next to his head, and, grabbing it by the neck, swung it squarely into the woman's temple. Her body immediately went slack and both orderlies pulled her backward from the doctor who, in turn, scuttled crablike backward from the fray, clutching at the remnants of his right ear, trying to staunch the flow of blood. He panted, wide-eyed, trying to reconcile what had just happened with the limp woman who now hung by her elbows between the two orderlies.

"Nellie … Nellie Bly! Wake up!" The nurse soundly slapped the woman's face.

The woman shuddered and blinked, blood flowing steadily over her eye, cheek, and closed lips from the fresh laceration on her forehead. The wide-eyed doctor cowered before her on the floor, his back against the wall.

"Time to go!" Nurse Pretorious waved a hand in front of her toward the orderlies. The woman smiled and shook her head, holding up one finger and pointing to the nurse's hand. The nurse raised an eyebrow and cautiously held her hand out. The woman spit into the nurse's hand, and the remnants of the doctor's bloody earlobe landed with a soft, wet plop in her palm.

Nurse Pretorious screamed and dropped the flesh to the floor as the orderlies dragged a still smiling Nellie Bly through the door.

Dr. Carandini crawled to pick up the chewed scrap of his ear and glanced up at Nellie. Her eyes twinkled. She gave him a playful, bloody grin and a wink.

Dr. Carandini gasped and looked to see if anyone

else had noticed, but he was the only witness. As she was dragged away, and the sounds of her giggling echoed in the halls, the doctor scrambled to retrieve the clipboard and fountain pen from amidst the chaos of the office floor.

Approval by Practicing Psychiatric Physician for Admittance to Bedlam Asylum:

He pressed his shaking hand to the page and signed "Carandini" below the other two signatures on the admittance page, leaving behind his bloody palm print for the record keeper's files.

CHAPTER 2

The bleak, gray sky stretched outward without end, so dense that not a single ray of light could penetrate the dull layers of cold and gloom. Where the clouds ended and the fog began was indiscernible. Nellie Bly sat on the wooden bench with her hands folded neatly in her lap. She would have liked to be able to rub her upper arms briskly to bring a scant bit of warmth to her chilled skin, but the handcuffs and trailing metal chain that secured her to the bench would not allow her hands to be farther than six inches apart.

Her editor at the Tribune had instructed her thusly:

"We do not ask you to go there for the purpose of making sensational revelations. Write up things as you find them, good or bad; give praise or blame as you think best, and as always, the truth all the time."

Before she left her desk at the Tribune, she had begun her exposé thusly.

It hadn't been an easy choice to make. Nellie Bly did not go undercover for every sensational story that an editor could dream up. In fact, I had initially had my reservations about embedding myself in such a place. But once I began to dig into the reasons behind the average admittance into Bedlam, the reason, quite often, did not have anything to do with a woman found to have mental instability. In fact, more often than not, Bedlam Asylum certainly seemed to be a dumping ground for women who were aged or homeless...their worst offense was being without means. Other offending admittances included upper-crust scoundrels who no longer wished to be married yet found divorce to be too messy and generally unaccepted by society at large. Once admitted to these so-called hospitals, the patients were often never to be seen or heard from again. Were they properly fed and clothed? Were they given a proper evaluation and treatment? Not only did I want to find the answers to these questions, I needed to know. Everyone needed to know. We are still looked down upon in the workforce. Our hard-earned wages have always been significantly lower than that of our male counterparts, regardless of our experience or knowledge. Women are expected to be satisfied in the realm of the home maker and nothing more. It sickens me that, to this day, men will not look beyond those meager boundaries. We have only just gained the right to vote and by God, there are many more battles ahead. This is why I must do this. Knowledge that is sought and kept selfishly but not shared eventually becomes nothing more than lost words and ideas. I seek to share all that I find in order to enlighten and thereby change the world. So that we, as women, will stand by each other. This exposé will reveal the truth, no matter how horrid, for I am in pursuit of only one result. Revolution.

Nellie made a mental note to begin her future and inevitable Pulitzer-prize winning editorial with the fact that, while one of the doctors had given her three quick stitches to staunch the flow of blood from her forehead, the orderlies who had escorted her away did not bother to cover her blood-stained dress with even a meager wrap to keep her from catching her death. Or perhaps, she might let that detail pass, as, with a smile, she surmised that they might not have wanted to remain within her proximity any longer than absolutely necessary. She listened to the rhythmic sloshing of the water against the creaking pier beneath her feet and shivered involuntarily, the damp chill air penetrating the thin, worn cloth of her dress. Nellie closed her eyes and began to compose a fresh sentence regarding her successful infiltration into the infamous Bedlam Asylum.

It surprised me how easy it was to convince the doctors and authorities that I was fit for the insane asylum that I was to be shipped off to.

Her concentration was broken by the sound of

the orderlies placing another person on the end of the bench. Glancing over, Nellie discovered that she would not be the only young patient to pass through the asylum doors today. There, on the opposite end of the bench, sat a frail, doe-eyed girl. The orderly attached her handcuffs to the bench and, with a solid tug on the chain, assured that her tethering was sound.

Nellie scowled. The inmates on the bench opposite her made sense. One wore an unusually large bonnet and muttered to herself, her weathered hands worrying at her tattered skirts. To that woman's side, and out of her reach, sat an older, thicker woman with a dress fashioned from bed ticking. Her silver hair stood on end and her continuous rocking back and forth was punctuated by occasional twitching. But the girl to Nellie's right did not at all fit into the story. She sat quietly, in a simple blue and white checked dress, with her hands resting in her lap. Someone had combed and parted her hair into two perfect braids and tied them with two perfect bows. From her rosy cheeks and pink full lips, down to her spotless, white ankle socks, this girl no more belonged in a mental institution than a mouse belonged in an alley full of cats. How could her parents do this to her? They must be monsters of some sort. Or perhaps insane themselves.

The waif struggled to smile at Nellie, but her red-rimmed, puffy eyes and tear-stained cheeks only served to make Nellie's heart even heavier. Nellie knew straightaway that she had another assignment: she must protect this vulnerable girl against the horrors they would both face very soon. Filled with furious resolve, Nellie would not abandon this girl the way the world clearly had. Nellie turned just enough to ensure that the orderlies and the head nurse would, upon looking over to the patients, see only the back of her head.

"Hello!" she whispered. The girl looked up at Nellie, her head tilted. "Can you hear me?" She nodded. "I'm Nellie. Nellie Bly."

The girl glanced over her shoulder. Nellie followed her gaze to the armed policemen who were deep in conversation with a woman in a black dress, white apron and cap. Her form was imposing, due not only to her unusual height and larger than average physique, but also to the thick, brown, leather belt slung about her waist. It was adorned with large, metallic, hypodermic syringes undoubtedly filled with sedatives designed to render unruly inmates immediately unconscious. Even armed with this formidable arsenal of chemicals, Nellie noted, this woman could most likely hold any offending patient in an arm-bar on her own, if needed, sedated or not.

"My uncle said we should all behave. And then we can get well," the girl murmured, still watching the nurse.

"What did they send you for?"

"I can see things. Things that — that hurt." She looked down into her lap again. A tear splashed onto her folded hands.

A powerful horn blast resonated throughout the dock, causing each person, standing or sitting, to jump. All except the head nurse, who motioned the policemen toward the patients anchored to their benches. The thick fog on the water formed tendrils that twisted and curled as though something monstrous was pushing through to make its way onto the pier to consume them all in its infinite cloak of gray.

It was not long after the echoes of the horn were lost to the sea that the shape of a dilapidated ferry became visible through the wall of thick, gray fog that lay along the outer harbor. The portly policeman with the bushy, brown mustache unlocked the girl's tethering chain and took her by the elbow.

"Get a move on, gussie. We ain't got all day." He yanked the youth from the bench, twisting her elbow sharply.

"Oh!" she cried out, wincing.

Nellie attempted to stand but instead was brought up short by her retaining chain and handcuffs. "Stop it! She's just a child! Can't you see you're hurting her?"

He caught the brunt of Nellie's fierce glare and his grip on the girl's arm loosened.

The other policemen appeared at Nellie's side and roughly secured her arms.

"Hey!" she yanked her arm out of the grip of the officer. "Why don't you pick on someone your own size?"

The head nurse caught Nellie's attention, as she appeared behind the policemen, holding aloft a syringe. She held Nellie's glare with steely, gray eyes and simply raised an eyebrow.

Nellie swallowed her fury, let her arms go slack in the grip of the policemen, and sat back down to stare silently out into nothingness. With a satisfied "humph," the head nurse returned the syringe to her belt.

Each patient walked, single-file, onto the banged-up, old ferry and into the dim cabin which stank of sweat and sick. A creaky, hard, wooden, bench lined the room, offering its patrons little more comfort than they would feel standing. The view out the dirty windows could hardly be described as such, with nothing but the dismal fog ahead.

The girl sat next to the mustachioed officer, and Nellie, next to her. Nellie and the girl looked out the open doorway to the dock and the swirling, dark water below. As the ferry began to move, and the pier slipped slowly away, the fog crept in on all sides to swallow the last glimpses of land.

Nellie suddenly had the oddest sensation of needing to flee before the dock disappeared completely. If she could quit these restraints, she would dash to the ferry's edge and leap, feet first, into the icy, dark water and then ... then what? Sink into the depths of this River Styx, struggling helplessly, as the water's surface closed over her head, the strength to fight sapped from her arms and legs, and watch the darkness above her fade to black.

No, there was no turning back now. The journey to Bedlam Asylum had begun.

Nellie watched the fog swallow the dock whole.

CHAPTER 3

T he only sound to compete with the low hum of the engine was the whispering rush of water against the sides of the decrepit ferry. Nellie inwardly composed the next paragraph of her exposé.

*We were to be shipped off to Bedlam Asylum —
some say the most infamous, highly-guarded asylum of
our time. With a dismissal record of rehabilitation, most
of Bedlam's patients never returned to society. Bedlam
became known as a place not only where souls go to
rest. But instead, where spirits go to die.*

Nellie was pulled abruptly from her thoughts by the sound of retching. On the seat next to her, her acquaintance in braids hunched over a bucket, loud and miserable from the motion. "Never been on a boat before?" Nellie whispered. The girl, now pale, looked sadly up to Nellie.

"Not really. We don't have a lot of them in Kansas."

Nellie placed her hand warmly on the girl's back. "Kansas? You're a long way from home."

Next to her, the mustachioed officer slumped against the wall with his arms folded. He breathed deeply, emitting the occasional soft snore. Across the cabin and next to the other new inmates sat the head nurse. She licked her thumb and turned the page of her newspaper.

"Not supposed to be here. They won't listen to me," the bonneted woman muttered, plucking unendingly at her skirt. The other woman continued, on the other side of the nurse, with her rocking and twitching, seemingly oblivious to her change of venue.

"What's your name, dear?" Nellie continued.

"Folks call me Dorothy." The queasy girl sat up

and leaned on Nellie's shoulder. An officer leaned across the snoring policeman next to Dorothy to hand them a tin cup with fresh, cold water. Nellie took the cup and held it out for Dorothy, but with one look into the cup, Dorothy lurched forward to return to the inner confines of the bucket.

Nellie dipped her fingers into the water and splashed it soothingly on Dorothy's neck and face. Dorothy turned to express her thanks, but her eye fell instead on the odd, dark-red spots that trailed down the front of Nellie's threadbare dress. She sat up weakly and leaned on one arm to point at Nellie's dress. "Nellie, is that — is that blood?"

Nellie nodded. She studied the girl's pale face and large brown eyes.

"You — you didn't hurt someone, did you?" she blinked to clear her long, wet eyelashes.

"Mostly myself." Nellie brought her handcuffs up as close to her head as her restraints would allow and pointed to the stiches above her eyebrow. "I had a bit of an accident."

"Oh," Dorothy nodded. "Is that why you're ... well, here?"

Nellie nodded. "Sometimes I don't know where I am or how I got there. It comes and goes."

"I see." Dorothy looked down into her lap. "Uncle Henry was really angry at me when the barn caught fire."

"A fire? Was everyone alright?"

"Yes. I told him it wasn't me. The Scarecrow did it. But he wouldn't listen. Nobody ever does." Dorothy stared at the floor.

"The Scarecrow did it?" Nellie followed Dorothy's intent gaze down to her shoes. Dorothy wore dazzling silver slippers, like nothing Nellie had ever seen before. In some places, the shoes were dull and streaked with red, while in other places they sparkled defiantly.

Dorothy waggled her feet back and forth. "Pigs' blood. That's what I got on my shoes. Right before the barn when it caught fire. I don't like blood," she sighed. "Not many people —"

The ferry horn blared so loudly that Nellie's teeth clacked together, and the mustachioed officer shot up from the bench with a harrumphing noise. They all turned to the window.

There it was. Bedlam Island.

CHAPTER 4

E verybody sit still. We're almost there." The head nurse folded her newspaper neatly and strode to the doorway of the ferry's cabin. Nellie peered through the window into the distance. The tendrils of fog twisted and curled again, this time gradually dissolving to reveal a small dock at the base of a rocky inlet with a black, pebbled shore. Dorothy did not move from her place on Nellie's shoulder, presumably still too sick to do anything but hope the journey to solid ground would end shortly. Two figures in dark-blue uniforms strode to the end of the dock to stand guard as the ferry made its slow approach. The officer who had offered up the tin of cold water rose from his seat on the bench and leisurely stretched, then slapped his mustachioed compatriot on the shoulder.

The nurse's voice floated in from the doorway to Nellie's attuned ears. "There are a couple of new patients onboard that should interest Dr. Braun."

"Up you go, girls," the officer next to Dorothy motioned toward the open door, watching Nellie. She noted that his hand rested on top of his billy club. Nellie waited with the others as, one by one, they shuffled out to the misty dock. Once again, the damp, bitingly-cold air seeped right through Nellie's threadbare dress and into her bones.

A white vehicle with four small windows appeared at the top of the hill. The words "Bedlam Asylum" arched over a circular logo, and, underneath, it read "AMBULANCE." One orderly in dark blue slammed a boarding ramp in place and the other ushered each new patient, by the elbow, into the box-shaped bus. The towering nurse was the last to be seated before the ramp was loaded back in and the solid back doors of the ambulance were shut with a sound slam. The officers retreated back into the ferry cabin. With a violent lurch and noxious belch of smoke, the ambulance began the journey to Bedlam Asylum.

The bonneted woman muttered to no one and stared at her feet as the ambulance swayed over steep slopes of tangled scrub grass that threatened to reintegrate the narrow tire grooves that wound their way between dense, leafless trees.

Dorothy, finally getting color back in her cheeks, craned her neck alongside Nellie to be able to peek out the windows. It wasn't long before the trees gave way to a clearing and they could see that the ambulance drove parallel to a broken-down iron and stone fence.

"That looks like a ..." Dorothy paused.

"Graveyard," Nellie whispered. It was not what either had expected to see on their way to a hospital meant to heal the insane. But, there it was, a number of broken and leaning headstones in a clearing overgrown with weeds, dead grass and leaves. Further on, the ambulance swung over a rocky knoll and began its descent past a towering, iron fence topped with jagged razor wire. The fence stretched out, curling and twisting in both directions as far as the eye could see.

"Oh my," Dorothy said, the color draining from her face once again.

"In case any of you are thinking of escaping, the fence is electrified," the nurse said with unnerving factuality. Nellie shot her an angry glance.

"If the shock doesn't stop you, the razor wire most certainly will," the nurse added and looked directly into Nellie's angry stare.

Dorothy's eyes filled with tears. "Is this real? I don't want this to be real!"

Nellie wanted to place an arm of solace over the weeping girl's shoulders, but instead she stared toward the window. She could feel the oppressive gaze of the nurse watching her every movement.

The ambulance ground to a halt in front of an enormous iron gate. Almost instantly, another uniformed orderly appeared from inside the grounds and with the distinct clang of metal on metal, he disengaged the lock. The heavy gate swung open with a groaning protest and ground to a halt in the crunching gravel.

The ambulance sputtered, and, with a loud backfire, pulled slowly forward. As the gate shut somewhere behind them, Nellie observed her new surroundings through the small windows of the ambulance. Rich, green, manicured lawns grew beneath great, sprawling trees punctuated by square hedges and bright, colorful flowers.

But the inmates living on the grounds stood in stark contrast to the grounds themselves; female inmates ranged in age from those in the prime of their youth to hunched and gnarled figures knocking at death's door. Each wore the same, shapeless gray dress. Most unsettling were their vacant stares as each, in turn, stopped in their tracks to watch the ambulance approach. Their eyes looked toward the ambulance's occupants but did not acknowledge them. Their eyes were empty; their faces, empty. Some of the women talked to no one at all. Others struggled futilely in their strait jackets as they were dragged along by impatient nurses.

The ambulance pulled up to the front of the enormous, granite building. It stood six stories tall with smooth stones and dormer windows streaked with sea salt and years of neglect. The sound of the ambulance doors opening and the boarding ramp being put into place must have been a familiar one. The asylum's windows filled with even more faces, some grotesquely distorted, pressing against the glass, all staring down at the new arrivals. The head nurse disembarked down the ramp, turned and waved for the new patients to follow. Nellie started down the ramp next, holding her handcuffed wrists out before her. Then she paused, took a deep breath, and glanced back up to the windows. They were all empty.

"Out! Out! Come on. We don't have all day." The head nurse waved Nellie toward her and tapped her foot. As Nellie took her place beside the nurse and Dorothy stooped to exit the ambulance, a line of patients shuffled past, each attached to the next by one long, thick strand of rope.

Nellie quickly sucked in her breath and held it; the gasp that had begun to escape her lips would surely have alerted the nurse, whose observation of Nellie's every movement was becoming oppressive.

"Inhumane," Nellie thought. She looked up again to the windows, troubled, but her thoughts were interrupted by an eerie wailing sound coming from somewhere above. A nurse cried out and pointed to the roof.

Perched impossibly high on a ledge on the asylum rooftop they saw a young woman. Her long, wavy, red hair whipped violently around her in the stiff ocean winds that buffeted the sixth floor. The girl's arms stretched outward as if to welcome the sky to her bosom.

"Alice will rise again!" she screamed into the harsh wind. "Alice! You promised ME eternal life in exchange for my soul!" She leaned toward the open air, stretching even farther toward her inevitable demise.

Dorothy put her shaking hands to her mouth, the chain of her handcuffs clinking with the trembling of her arms.

"I'm here to do your bidding!" the girl cried. She began to fall slowly forward. "I will —" The red head quite suddenly disappeared in a flurry of movement as several orderlies and nurses yanked her back from the ledge.

"No!!! You cannot make me!" the blood-curdling screech carried on the ocean wind down to the courtyard below.

"Yes, yes they can," whispered someone near Nellie.

Nellie turned quickly to find the whisperer. All around her, patients hunched over, moaning and trying to hide in their hands. "She's not real ... Alice is not real ...." Moans echoed from the grounds around her. Others fell to the ground to curl up into protective balls and weep. "She's coming back ... she's coming back ... Alice is coming back ...." The whispers and wails surrounded Nellie.

An inmate with snow-white hair and gnarled hands dropped to her knees. "I didn't do it, Alice. I was a good girl!" She clawed at her eyes, drawing blood and tearing flesh from her face. She screamed at the top of her lungs, "I promise I was good! Leave me alone!" A nurse appeared at her side and struggled to pin the patient's arms and save what was left of her eyes.

Nellie stood rooted to the spot, not daring to move, as the pandemonium around her worsened. "Who ... was that? The roof ... Who is Alice?"

"ALIIIIICCCEEEE!!!" howled the inmates, clawing at their ears and falling to the ground.

"What in the name of —" Nellie breathed, spinning around.

"Nellie?"

Nellie turned back around just in time to see Dorothy's eyes roll up into her head and her faint form crumple to the gravel walkway. The head nurse shoved her sleeves up her arms and pulled a whistle from her pocket.

*TWEEEEEEEEEEEEEEEEEEEEEEEEEEEEEEEEE
EEEEEETTTTTTTTT!*

The sharp penny-whistle sounded throughout the courtyard and carried across the lawn with immediate effect. Patients dropped their arms, returned to upright positions and began to shuffle and mill about as if nothing had happened at all.

"Alright, the show is over!" The head nurse turned back toward Nellie and motioned for another caretaker to quit her current charge and instead assist the prostrate Dorothy back to consciousness. As the young nurse waved smelling salts under Dorothy's nose and patted her tear-stained cheek, the head nurse motioned to Nellie.

"Follow me. Dr. Braun would like to see you."

Dorothy blinked and took a shuddering breath. With a sigh of relief, Nellie turned her attention back to the windows to look for the crush of inmates that had been there just minutes before. All of the dark windows were empty. All except one.

There, in a dormer window, a small figure looked back at her. Nellie's breath caught. The girl was slight, her face covered by stringy, blond hair. Her gray dress covered in dark red spatters hung down shapeless from her shoulders. The hair on Nellie's arms stood up, her blood turning to ice. The girl's face ... Nellie could not see her face. Where one would expect to see features or some form of familiar visage, there was no form, just pale, white nothingness, a masque of death. The small form vanished backward into the darkness. Nellie stumbled backward the strength drained from her legs.

"Hurry up! What's wrong with you?" the head nurse chided, impatiently.

Her heart pounding, Nellie searched the window again. The little girl was gone without a trace. The head nurse wrapped her long, bony fingers around Nellie's upper arm and simultaneously lifting and dragging her along, her iron grip pulling Nellie off her feet as the nurse strode toward the building entrance. The nurse behind them had brought the shaken Dorothy to her feet and they took small, fleeting steps to keep up with the head nurse's great strides. The gate buzzed long and loud. Nellie and Dorothy were pulled roughly across the threshold and into Bedlam Asylum. The gate slammed shut behind them and the sound echoed eerily throughout the many halls of the vast madhouse.

CHAPTER 5

W elcome to Bedlam Asylum," the head nurse's
crisp voice cut through the thick, musty air.

At last, Nellie began her first reporter's assessment
of Bedlam. The last rays of afternoon sunlight broke
through stained window panes and revealed the
building's age and neglect. Dirty, gray paint had
chipped and peeled from the walls, leaving large cracks
that exposed the brickwork beneath. The tiled floors,
had, at one time, been checked with cheerful, bright
white, and rich, black squares, but the white had
become so dingy, and the black so worn away, that both

colors of tile were now nearly the same gray that barely adorned the decaying walls.

Patients moved through the dreary halls, dragging their feet, shuffling endlessly to and fro without purpose or destination. One such patient reached the far wall, and, without pause for problem solving, bumped repeatedly into the wall. Dorothy's nurse left her side to offer the inmate assistance, gently turning the patient until she faced the opposite direction and began her shuffling journey, back the way she had come.

And so I have reached the end of the world. Here it is. Where it all begins. And where it will all end.

A flight of stairs rose up before them, separating the east and west wings. One piece of décor seemed completely out of place in this massive gray stone pit of despair. On the wall next to the stairs hung an ornate looking mirror, of such exquisite detail that Nellie found herself drawn toward it for a closer examination. It was of a make from a century before, its decaying, antique, gold frame intricately etched with petal patterns encircled by curling gold scrollwork. As Nellie examined the scrollwork more closely at the top of the frame, a hidden detail revealed itself: a golden skull had been cleverly worked into the elaborate frame design. Nellie's gaze shifted from the curious frame to the looking glass itself. There, reflected back at her, were the peeling walls, the dingy floor, and Nellie standing before the glass, her hands still handcuffed together as she awaited admittance. Something was not right.

Nellie whipped around, looking left and right. There was the head nurse, speaking with an orderly, and only a little further away was Dorothy. Against the wall, a woman stood, hunched over and muttering, while another moved slowly toward the east wing. Two orderlies passed behind her.

Nellie turned sharply back to the mirror and her stomach lurched. Only she was reflected; no one else. She closed her eyes and counted to three, then opened them again. The reflection remained the same, even as another patient passed behind her and down the hall. Then, in the reflection, the main door to Bedlam began, gradually, to swing open.

Nellie glanced over her shoulder to the actual door behind her and verified that it was indeed shut. Yet, back in mirror's reflection, it was unmistakably opening. Nellie held her breath. From the darkness beyond the door, a face emerged — a small, pale face that could not be seen through the mass of stringy, dirty, blond hair.

Nellie gasped and stumbled back from the mirror and its deceitful reflection. She, again, looked over her shoulder to the actual door. It was shut. The head nurse continued her conversation with the orderly. Dorothy leaned against the wall, wiping away the occasional tear.

Nellie looked back into the mirror and cried out. There stood the little girl, in front of the backward reflection of the open door. Her arms hung limply at the sides of her tattered, gray dress, still spattered with dark-red matter. Her grimy hair hung thickly over her face and shoulders.

The girl stood motionless.

"What is the matter with you?" the head nurse

exclaimed, pulling her up sharply as Nellie stumbled backward. "You are really starting to get on my nerves!"

Nellie gasped and pointed to the mirror, unable to find words.

"Are you afraid of your own reflection?" the head nurse asked.

Nellie prepared to fire back a less than gracious reply before she realized that this was a perfectly reasonable question for someone of her supposed state of mind. She simply shook her head.

"Well, what then?" the nurse gestured toward the mirror.

Nellie followed her sweeping hand and looked into the mirror again to see only her own reflection and that of the head nurse, who was assessing her with a raised eyebrow. Nellie blinked and checked again. Nothing.

"Enough nonsense. Time to go." The head nurse nodded, and motioned to a waiting nurse and an orderly. They each took Nellie and Dorothy by an arm and led them out of the room, leaving the bonneted patient and the elderly woman in the bed-ticking dress in the care of another nurse.

Nellie glanced once more over her shoulder to the mirror, but saw only her own confused reflection staring back. Another buzzer sounded and the orderly unlocked a wooden door followed by a barred fence.

"Good afternoon, Miss Tilley," the head nurse nodded to a blond woman in the starched, white cap and uniform of Bedlam Asylum. The admittance nurse sat in a squeaky chair behind the counter of the room into which they had just been ushered.

"Good afternoon, Ms. Ball," the light haired nurse nodded back. "Committal sheet?" She pulled out a long, white paper and accepted a few file folders from the head nurse.

"Nurse Ball" — so this was the staunch head nurse's name.

"You will leave all of your valuables here in this room," Nurse Ball addressed both new inmates.

Nellie reached into her pocket and placed its contents on the counter in front of Nurse Tilley.

"Three pen nibs. One ten-penny piece. One bunch of keys on a single black, metal ring." She wrote each item on a report as she listed them aloud, and then placed them in box labeled "BLY".

"Anything else?"

Nellie shook her head, but the orderly gave her a gentle pat-down to assure that Nellie was being truthful.

"Sign here, please." Nurse Tilley slid the bottom of the form over to the edge of the counter and held out a fountain pen for Nellie. Nellie signed her name to the committal sheet.

Dorothy placed her red-stained, silver slippers on the counter.

Nurse Tilley frowned. "That's it?"

Dorothy nodded. "That's all I have." Her eyes brimmed with tears and she took the fountain pen from Nurse Tilley.

I hereby commit myself voluntarily to the treatment which has been explained to me including the types of medication and examination procedures for psychiatric treatment. I understand that in order to leave before I am discharged I must have the consent of my psychiatric physician and at least 72 hours' notice in writing to those in charge of my treatment. I confirm that my rights and responsibilities while a patient in this hospital have been explained to me.

A tear escaped her brimming eyes to slide down her red cheek and spatter the long white form, where the young girl's trembling hand penned her name.

Dorothy Gale

Nurse Tilley pulled the form away from Dorothy, nodded, and averted her eyes.

The paperwork having been officially signed, stamped, and processed, it was time for the doctor's official evaluation. Nellie was curious to see what sort of treatment the doctor would recommend for her "ailment", and particularly that of the vulnerable young Dorothy. They sat on a stiff bench outside of the doctor's office and awaited their appointments with the asylum physician, the cries of the insane interjecting occasionally into their quiet conversation. Dorothy used the edge of her newly-adorned, shapeless, gray dress to dab at her eyes and nose.

"Don't cry. It's going to be okay." Nellie patted Dorothy's hand.

"I'm scared."

Nellie looked into Dorothy's watery, brown eyes and smoothed down a few of the dark, brown hairs around her face that had begun to unravel from her braids. "That's what they want. They want you to be weak and afraid. But you have to be strong, alright?"

"That's easy for you to say. I'm not brave like you, Nellie."

"You're braver than you think."

The doctor's heavy, wooden door swung open. Nurse Ball partially emerged, holding a clipboard. "Dorothy Gale?" she motioned to the frail girl. Dorothy stood uncertainly and looked once more back to Nellie. Nellie leaned back, out of Nurse Ball's view, and smiled to Dorothy.

"You'll be fine."

Dorothy stepped into the office door and Nurse Ball closed it behind them, but not without first carefully regarding Nellie. Nellie, however, had already obligingly painted a slack-jawed emptiness on her face and was fully engaged in examining the emerald green hue of the wall. Satisfied, Nurse Ball shut the door with a click.

Nellie felt a sharp poke in her upper arm.

"You saw her."

"Ow! Hey!" Nellie's head whipped back around to face the perpetrator of the painful jab. Standing over her, reed-like, was the pale, red-headed adolescent from the rooftop. Her long, unkempt red hair was full of knots and tangles and was held loosely back by a dirty, blue bow that scarcely clung to her head. Her sickly pallor was softened only by plethora of brown freckles that adorned her nose and cheeks. She swayed as if caught in an invisible breeze.

"What are you talking about?" Nellie rubbed the throbbing point on her arm that surely would turn into a fingertip-sized bruise.

"You've seen Alice." The look in the girl's eyes

gave Nellie a sensation like an icy finger trailing down her back.

Nellie scooted a few inches away. "Who?"

The girl cocked her head to one side to listen to something to which Nellie was not privy.

Nellie found herself oddly fascinated, yet wary. She studied the girl's face. "Alice? Who is she?" Nellie queried.

The girl looked abruptly back to Nellie and grinned. "She's Bedlam! She's everywhere ...." After a moment of reflection, the youth trailed off into her world again.

Nellie thought for a moment. *How does one make sense out of nonsense?* "Why is everyone so afraid of her?" she asked.

The girl looked instantly back at Nellie, eyes flashing with anger. She threw her hands up in the air and leapt up onto the bench with a thud. She pointed at Nellie, her fingertip within an inch of Nellie's nose. "Stay away from Alice!" she hissed. "Are you listening to me? Stay away!"

Nellie didn't dare move, but her body tensed to flee if it became necessary.

"Once she gets inside your head, you're

FINISHED!" The girl leaned into Nellie's face, her head swaying left and right.

Nellie remained still. Their faces were so close that she could see the flecks of gold in the girl's wild blue eyes.

An iron key scraped in the office door's lock and Nellie turned, hopeful that Dorothy would emerge unscathed. Instead she was met with shock when orderlies on either side of Dorothy carried the limp girl out of the office, her head lolling to one side. Nellie stood to reach out to Dorothy, but the orderlies brushed her aside.

"What have they done to her?" Nellie fumed. This was not a girl who needed sedation of any sort.

"Dr. Braun will see you now." Nurse Ball held the office door for Nellie. "WALK!" she loudly addressed to the red-haired girl who hummed and skipped down the hall away from them. Yet the youth continued her humming and skipping, leaving the unheeded Nurse Ball to "tsk, tsk" to herself. Jaw set, and fists clenched, Nellie turned and stepped through the door and into the doctor's office, ready for the worst.

CHAPTER 6

*I*t was a full moon. Even in the dead of a warm summer night, the moonlight was bright enough for Dorothy to find her way through the cornfield without a lantern. But the lantern wasn't swinging from her hand because she needed it to see. She kept it with her because she didn't trust him. She tiptoed through the tall, green stalks of corn that rustled and swayed in the cool breeze. All around her, as far as she could see, tiny green lights flickered through the air as lightning bugs flashed their greetings to one another. She moved cautiously through the field, listening to crickets chirping and frogs croaking. It had only been a few days since their newest sow gave birth to her first litter *of piglets, so Dorothy had taken it upon herself to check in on them now and again. Tonight, she couldn't sleep, so it seemed as good a time as any to check in on the mother and her babies.*

She stopped and used her free hand to part the stalks of corn in front of her. Yes, there was the silhouette of the red barn and the big, full moon seeming to hang just behind its roof.

The crickets and frogs fell silent. Dorothy held her breath and listened — nothing.

She turned the knob of her lantern down almost as far as it could go starving the flame inside nearly to death, it struggled to hold on to life with the merest deep blue flicker. She turned, quickly parted the corn behind her, and stood on tip toe to peer just above the tops of the plants, toward the other end of the field.

It was still there. Its black form hung limply in the shape of a crucifix, arms draped over a rough-hewn wooden pole. Again she held her breath — nothing. She moved cautiously forward, through the tall, green stalks, careful not to make a sound.

"Dorothy," the wind whispered. She froze.

"Who's there?" She lifted her lantern high and searched, but no one answered. "Just the wind," she murmured, and pushed through the cornstalks toward the barn.

Something rustled in the corn behind her.

"Hello?" Dorothy stopped and stood up on tip-toe again to see over the tops of the vibrant green stalks.

The wooden pole, where he had hung just a few minutes before, was now empty. Dorothy stepped back and lost her footing. She cried out as she fell backward through the thick rough corn stalks behind her. Her lantern dropped from her hand, and, extinguishing with a hiss, rolled a few inches away into the darkness at the base of the corn stalks.

Dorothy reached swiftly into her nightgown pocket to pull out a small box of matches. Holding it up to the moonlight, peeping through the tops of the tall corn stalks, she slid the small box open and fumbled for one of the thick matches. Dorothy dragged the match head quickly over the emery surface of the box. The flame burst to life with bright, orange light and the smell of sulfur. Carefully, she knelt back down on the musty dump earth in the darkness. In the soft light of the match's flame, she found the lantern once again. Lifting the lantern's glass hood, she touched the match flame to the burnt cream cloth of the wick.

A small gust rustled the cornstalks around her. The match flame went out.

"No, no, no, no ...." Dorothy's hand started to shake. She felt around in her pocket for the matchbox. Now, her legs felt rooted to the spot and she did not want to stand. She slid the box open and fished out a second match. She snapped the match smartly across the side of the box igniting the head. As the match hissed its first breath of light and life, she brought it down to the lantern's wick.

A sudden, concentrated, hot puff of air blew directly into Dorothy's face, blowing her long, dark hair back as it extinguished the life she held in her hand. She sat on her heels, listening. Trembling.

A low-throated, gravelly resonance issued from

somewhere next to her. The sound lifted the hairs on Dorothy's arms and neck, striking raw fear within her. It was not unlike the threatening growl of a crouched dog before an attack. But there was no earthly creature that could make such a deep, preternatural sound. The strong scent of sulfur wafted around her, overpowering the comforting smell of rich, fertile soil. She gagged and wretched.

"BE GONE WITH YOU!" she shrieked, and shoved the glass back onto the lantern. The glass of the lantern rattled in her shaking hands.

The low-throated sound issued forth again, this time from the darkness just next to her. It was almost a chuckle. The moist heat of rotten breath tickled her ear. Without thought, she leapt to her feet. The house was much closer than the barn, so she ran, as fast as her feet could carry her, back toward the safety of the farm house.

The cornstalks next to her rapidly flattened as something loped through the field parallel to her. Dorothy dodged away on a diagonal path, unable to see where she was headed, but hoping her new direction would carry her away from the thing pursuing her. Her heart beat as if it would burst out of her chest, and she struggled for breath. Her mind was a flurry of electric shock telling her, only on the basest of levels, that she must run for her life. There was the house! Just a little further and —

From directly in front of her came a sudden torrent of noise and movement burst forth. It rose up before Dorothy, screeching, a deadly twister teaming with darkness and screeching. A murder of cawing crows swirled and flew upward, a whirlwind of black. The sound of demonic laughter was barely audible just beyond the cacophony that blocked her path.

Without thought or hesitation, she had sprung in the opposite direction, back through the corn, toward the other possible refuge: the big red barn. From the back of her mind, Dorothy watched herself running, pell-mell, toward the looming red structure. She could not feel the cornstalks lashing her arms, legs, and face as she flew, but they left miniscule, razor-thin cuts that oozed fine streaks of blood across her exposed skin.

Dorothy erupted from the last row of corn, the small, hard pebbles beneath her slippers crunching as she pounded across the path to the big, red, double doors with white trim. She grasped the barn door handle with her free hand and, with the herculean strength of fight or flight, threw one door open, ducked inside, and slammed it shut again.

She was greeted by the sounds of hogs snoring in their pens and horses chuffing quietly in their stalls. A large square of blue-white moonlight shone on the hay-strewn plank floor. Dorothy knelt in the patch of moonlight and quickly went to work retrieving a new match from her pocket. Striking it firmly across the emery, she used its life to bring new light to the lantern. Once the ghost of the blue flame appeared, she cranked the lantern knob all the way up and illuminated her immediate surroundings with the bright yellow light of the unrestrained lantern flame.

The roof creaked. Dorothy swung around and lifted the full power of the lantern to bear on the source of the sound. Her eyes wide, she stood silently and listened. A horse stood and pawed at the ground with a soft whinny.

Silence.

Dorothy spun back around and lifted the lantern toward the hayloft. A black shadow moved. Misshapen and low to the hayloft floor, the shadow slunk and retreated from the light. Or had the darkness swallowed up the light?

Dorothy gulped, and, struggling to suppress the quaking in her voice, exclaimed, "I am NOT afraid of you!" Did she mean it, or was she just trying to convince herself?

She listened, staring holes into the place where she had last seen the shadow move. From somewhere on the floor ahead of her, the low, rumbling, unearthly chuckle answered her. Her shaking was uncontrollable. The light from her lantern jiggled across the barn walls, creating an array of shadows crawling up the walls and across the ceiling behind her. She stared hard toward the unearthly sound, determined to gain back control.

Two glowing, red embers peered back at her. After a few moments, they disappeared.

A scream came from her left.

"NO!" she cried out and swung her lantern toward the hog pen. With a squeal, like that of a small girl screaming, one of the hogs was lifted from its pen, the sound of ripping and tearing quickly silencing the animal. With a hard, wet splat, the dead hog landed at Dorothy's feet. She quickly stumbled back, still holding her lantern. The new mother hog's blood gushed from its nearly severed head and pooled on the floor, the puddle growing larger and larger as it rolled toward her silver slippers. She shuffled quickly backward, the toes of her slippers just an inch away from the growing pool of blood. The sow's tongue lolled and its eyes rolled back in its head. Its body jerked abruptly as the vile thing in the darkness tore pieces of the hog away.

"How dare you ... how dare you ..." Dorothy's raw fear began to take an altogether different shape. She

had retreated as far as she could and now her back touched the barn wall. There was nowhere else to go.

She looked from the dead, white eyes of the hog back down to the toes of her favorite, sparkling, silver shoes. Poor mother. The warm hog's blood oozed forward and rolled over the tips of the shoes that sparkled in the lantern light. The sparkles slowly consumed by the thick blood, the light on her shoes ceased to dance.

Defiled. That thing had tainted the one treasure a poor farm girl could call truly her own.

"How could you ...." She said through gritted teeth.

The newborn piglets cried softly from the pen for their mother.

"How DARE you ...." Dorothy growled, the ice in her arms melted, turning to heat. Her blood began to boil. The fear in her stomach drained. She stared at her shoes — at the blood that ran along the sides and swallowed the silver sparkle that gave them life. The rage swallowed her fear whole.

The chuckling came again. Before her, the blackness

that crouched over the viscera of the dead hog began to rise. Its lanky, thin form unwound, stretching impossibly high as it stood. Its red eyes shone in the darkness, watching her. She could see its face aglow with a soft, blue light. Its lips dripped blood, as the corners of its mouth stretched and cracked its dead, yellowed skin into a smile that ran from ear to ear, revealing rotting, pointed teeth covered in red.

"Go away ..." Dorothy commanded, her fists clenching. She raised the lantern by the handle and then gripped it, hot glass and all, in her palms. She could not, or would not, feel anything now. "GO AWAY!" she shouted.

The thing stood fifteen feet tall before her, throwing open its arms, its hands spattering fresh blood on her white nightgown. It began to laugh, taking one long stride, over the hog's corpse, toward her. Dorothy pitched the lantern at the creature, shattering it across the monster's chest. The fiend howled and burst into flame, the lantern oil covering it and catching fire. It threw its hands up and stumbled. But, even as the flames licked at its skin and tattered clothing, it hunched over and screeched, its red eyes locking with Dorothy's. She could see its rage. It sprang at her, dropping fiery remnants as it went. Flames sprang up in the pen and the stalls from the trail of fire the creature left as it strode toward Dorothy.

Dorothy was no longer afraid. In defiance of the monster before her, she stood her ground. Her hair rose up around her head, lifted by some supernatural wind. She held her arms away from her sides; she could feel the rage flowing through her like blood through her veins.

The tall creature took another long stride and Dorothy was almost within its grasp. But it was Dorothy who closed the distance. She leapt from the wall and strode toward the impossibly tall monstrosity now engulfed in flame. With her arms held out before her, she willed the creature backward with her hate. It fell to the floor — and laughed even louder. Its deep, gurgling chortles reverberated off the barn walls and ceiling.

Around them the hogs squealed and the horses bucked and kicked. The terrified animals squealed and fought against their restraints, desperate to find a way to escape the quickly spreading flames. Dorothy leapt onto the creature sprawled across the entire barn floor. She grasped at the head and scratched and clawed as it continued to laugh, its wild eyes now visibly yellow and rimmed with red in the fire-lit room.

Filled with hatred and rage, she thrust her hand claw-like through the dry, taut, dead skin that stretched across the top of its head and grasped at the viscera within, pulling out handfuls of reddish-black, dripping pieces of flesh and hay — things that had once been the various organs of other creatures. The beast's yellow and red eyes rolled up into its head and the laughter melted into gurgling. Its blackening body split and cracked with the heat of the flames.

"DOROTHY!" A man's voice broke through the clouds of thick smoke that surrounded her. Her fixation broken, she looked up and realized that the searing, hot smoke in the barn was too thick for her to see anything.

The blue light had vanished. Dorothy was lost, blind, and barely able to breath in the thick, black smoke.

"Uncle Henry!" Dorothy tried to call back, coughing and spluttering. From out of the darkness, two strong arms gripped her and she felt herself sliding away from the barn. A few moments later, she breathed in sweet, cool, fresh air. Both of her uncles ran back into the barn and, a moment later, the horses and hogs came running through the door and out into the yard.

"Dorothy!" cried her Aunt Em, running to the girl, who was lying limply on the grass.

"I'm alright, I'm alright, Auntie Em!" Dorothy hiccupped. She felt the relief of a cold wet towel on her neck as her Aunt Em attended to her. Only now did she acknowledge the dull, throbbing pain in her palms where she had burned them on the lantern's glass.

With a loud crack, a portion of the barn's roof collapsed. "Uncle Henry! Hunk!" Dorothy screamed. Aunt Em gripped Dorothy's shoulders with worry and watched the barn door, willing her husband and the farmhand to appear. Uncle Henry jumped out the door, followed by Hunk, both of them coughing and spluttering. Dorothy took a shuddering breath of relief and collapsed.

"... I slipped on the hog's entrails," she heard, too weak to open her eyes. There was a sharp intake of breath. That was Aunt Em.

"What — what has she done, Henry?" There was a moment's hesitation before Uncle Henry could answer.

"She ... uh ... she ... well, she musta tore that hog apart with her bare hands." There was a hiccup and a sob.

"But she's just a child!" Aunt Em openly wept. Hot tears splashed onto Dorothy's face.

"Em, it could be one of us next. You don't know what she's capable of." Uncle Henry's voice broke. Dorothy had never heard Uncle Henry cry before.

"Ya gotta do it now, Miss Em." Hunk's voice came from her side. "She's got to be committed. She's a danger to everyone, even herself."

Dorothy struggled to speak, but was too weak to rouse herself from her near catatonia. "Let's get her in the house." Aunt Em's shaking voice could be heard over the clanging bell of the approaching fire brigade.

Dorothy felt herself hoisted up onto one shoulder of her frail Aunt and one shoulder of strong Uncle Henry, the toes of her once sparkling shoes dragging across the pebbled path back toward the farmhouse. Summoning all her strength, she opened her eyes.

There was the field. There was the burning barn and the clanging, red, fire truck. She could hear the fire chief shouting for someone to find the well. There were the wandering hogs and horses. And there, in the cornfield, dangling from its wooden cross, was the Scarecrow, silhouetted and perfect against the moon.

CHAPTER 7

H ave a seat," the doctor behind the desk said, with a wave of his pen. Dr. Braun's thick-lensed spectacles perched precariously on the tip of his bulbous nose. When he finally glanced up to look at Nellie, she was struck by the urge to laugh but suppressed it with a cough instead. His thick lenses made the pale eyes in his pale, wrinkled face look large and fish-like.

The sun's rays streamed in from the window highlighting his silvery-gray hair and beard. Where Nellie had expected to find the usual framed certificates and medical achievements on the wall behind his desk, there were instead shelves containing preserved biological specimens and disturbing devices whose purposes were not readily apparent. There were rough sketches of machines. One, in particular, was pinned next to a photo of a completed project that appeared to be a bed of some sort, yet it had all manner of wires and straps. The only personal item anywhere was a photo of a smiling young girl standing next to a beautiful woman with black hair.

"Nellie Bly, is it?" Dr. Braun pushed the spectacles back up the bridge of his nose and leaned forward to study her while she surveyed the oddities adorning his office wall.

"That's me," she said, peering at another odd photo of the doctor posing proudly next to a human-sized square, metal contraption with hoses and gauges.

"Tell me, Nellie. Do you have any acquaintances in the area?" Nellie looked from the wall to the doctor.

"Is this a new measurement of sanity? How many people are in my social circle?" she thought. But she was here to get answers, not give them, so on with the charade.

Nellie pulled what appeared to be a fetal cat in a jar closer to her and peered through the glass. "This is certainly the strangest pickle I have ever seen." The doctor put his hand atop the jar and pulled it back.

"Any friends? Family perhaps?" he continued.

"Yes. Here, kitty, kitty!" Nellie said as she slid the jar back her way, seemingly lost in the grotesqueness of the half-formed kitten's face.

Dr. Braun stood, picked up the jar, and thunked it down on a shelf, where the creature sloshed back and forth in its formaldehyde home.

"Oh!" Nellie exclaimed, slapping her hands on the edge of his desk. "Is this to be my examination?"

He leaned across the desk, closing the distance between them. "I ask the questions, Ms. Bly, not you. Do you have any living relatives?"

Nellie grinned. "I told you I did. Is that important? If you find me sane, do I get to return home 'to my relatives'?" She clapped her hands with delight and leaned back in the rickety wooden chair.

The doctor's pale face began to flush with color. He

glanced to Nurse Ball and set his jaw. "Answer the question, Ms. Bly. Who are your living relatives? Where do they live?"

Nellie leaned forward and pointed to the photo of the doctor next to the metallic box. "Oh, is that an iron lung?" She jumped up out of the chair and touched the photo. "Or is it perhaps some kind of humongous jack-in-the-box?"

Dr. Braun's nostrils flared, and he motioned to Nurse Ball with a stiff finger. Nurse Ball took Nellie by the elbow and sat her, forcefully, back down into her chair. "Go on, Nellie. Tell the doctor what he wants to know." She placed her hand on Nellie's shoulder and pressed firmly. This was clearly not just a suggestion.

Nellie looked from the doctor to the window. "Well I am just wondering what a doctor who heals the mentally ill would be doing with all of these contraptions and ..." she waved her hands toward the specimens, " ... these things. Yuck."

The doctor snatched his spectacles from his face and polished them on his jacket. Nurse Ball turned away to give the appearance of looking out the window, but Nellie caught Nurse Ball's reflection in the glass and saw the secret smile she tried to hide from view.

Dr. Braun forced an unconvincing smile and sat back down opposite Nellie in his chair behind the desk. "You'll learn one thing very quickly here. We have all the time in the world."

"Oh, so do I, good doctor!" Nellie retorted, and returned the attempted smile. "I am just waiting for you to ask me a question that actually pertains to my mental state."

The doctor's face flushed. He whipped his spectacles onto the bridge of his nose and jabbed a finger toward Nellie. "You will answer whatever questions I see fit to ask!"

Nellie stood and curtly nodded. "In that case, Doctor, I believe we have reached an impasse."

Dr. Braun snapped the book in his hand shut and gave Nurse Ball a sharp nod. "Very well — send her for decontamination and put her in Block D."

Nurse Ball opened the office door and summoned two waiting orderlies to escort Nellie out of the room.

"What? That was my evaluation?" It was Nellie's turn to become red-faced as the orderlies took her by the arms and forcibly scooted her toward the door.

"We will finish this conversation another time, when you are ready to cooperate." Dr. Braun leaned back in his chair and picked up a fresh medical evaluation sheet for review.

Nurse Ball stood before Nellie, her disapproving glare speaking volumes.

"Are you going to go quietly like your friend? Or are you going to be a problem?" Her fingertips rested lightly on the top of a full syringe hanging from the brown, leather belt slung about her waist.

"A problem!" Nellie stated, with a single nod to illustrate her unwavering confirmation of that fact. "This is unjust! This is negligence!" Nellie dug her heels into the floor, fighting the orderlies' attempts to pull her from the room.

Dr. Braun smirked. "So you're a lawyer now, too?"

"So you're a 'doctor,' you say?" Nellie retorted, yanking her arm out of the grasp of an orderly. She couldn't help herself any longer. Dr. Braun nodded to Nurse Ball, who solemnly bowed her head in acknowledgement.

"Well, that tore it," Nellie thought sourly, struggling to step out of range of the syringe Nurse Ball had pulled from her belt. Suddenly, a hot, sharp pain filled Nellie's upper- right arm as the nurse injected her with the sickly-looking brown liquid. Nellie could feel the chemical heat of the drug in her veins as it rushed down to her fingertips, into her legs, and back up her left side. Within seconds, Nellie's vision blurred, and the light in the room shrank to a pinpoint. She felt immediately sick to her stomach, and then moments later, lost control over her own limbs. Nurse Ball sighed heavily, as the orderlies slung Nellie's arms over their necks and proceeded to drag yet another sedated woman out of Dr. Braun's office.

CHAPTER 8

N ellie awoke to find herself standing in a long, dark corridor. Rusted, metal pipes lined the walls, and the stink of must and mold invaded her senses, aggravating her already intense nausea. She struggled to make sense of where she stood. Cold, damp, cement under her feet. Cement walls dripping with streaks of dark orange and red rust. Nellie swayed and struggled to bring her hand up to the wall for support. Where was the light at the end of this corridor? Was she in a basement somehow?

Pipes groaned and hissed. The sounds of laughter

echoed down the corridor ... not jovial. This was the sound of the unhinged.

An iron door slammed shut. A bleating animal cried out. Nellie put her hand to her head; it felt three feet thick. Something skittered across the stone floor in front of her. Nellie closed her eyes and opened them again hoping to clear away the darkness. Surely this could not be happening?

A small, white rabbit stood in the hall ahead, on top of some scattered, yellowed papers that littered the floor, its paws crossed over one another. One ear stood upright while the other flopped over. Most curiously, it wore a mask. The mask was of a human face, yet it was blank.

"What are you doing here?" Nellie said, blinking sluggishly. The fuzzy, detached feeling from the medication made it so difficult to think.

The rabbit cocked its head. With one solid stomp of its foot, it turned and hopped down the corridor into the darkness. Nellie scooped up a few of the forgotten pages to examine them more closely

The Basement

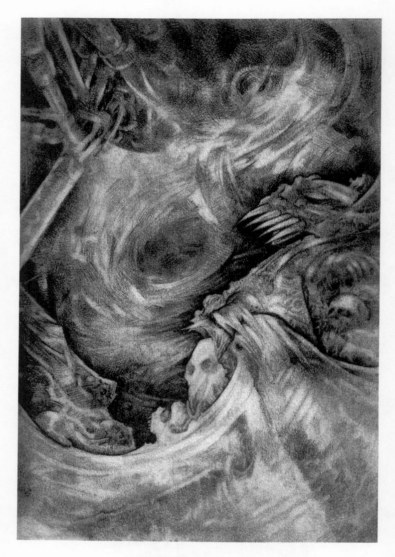

THE BREAKING

Faceless In The Shadows

The pages Nellie scooped up from the floor contained disturbing illustrations that had been rendered by scratching and smearing charcoal. Nellie decided that these images must be from one of the other patients of Bedlam, some form of art therapy. One page depicted a yawning, black pit with the souls and shadows of the lost and forgotten. They reached upward toward the one source of light, an open door that they could never reach. Another page swirled and flowed with demonic creatures, claws tearing, ghostly apparitions, skulls, phantoms, decay, and faces of death. Nellie realized that the more she examined the drawing, the more it revealed to her. There were pictures inside the pictures: a cat atop a ravenous demon, a screaming face within a phantom's veil ... all caught up in a vortex, swirling toward ... toward what? The closer she got, the more she found the madness within the madness.

She pulled the third page forward to examine the next set of visceral imagery, but a faraway, off-key humming caught her ear. She quietly lowered the pages and turned her head toward the humming. To her surprise, words followed.

Why doth the little insane child
Improve her shining blade,
To spill the blood of those that smiled
Then left her so betrayed.
How very cross she has become,
The madness can't be stopped,
Although salvation waits for some,
The rest must all be chopped.

SCREEEEEEEEEEEEEEEEAAAAAKKKKKKKK!

Nellie squeezed her eyes shut, dropped to her knees, and pressed her hands tightly over her ears. The papers fluttered back to the floor around her. That sound! It was unbearable, like fingernails across slate. It just kept going and going, getting louder and LOUDER. No — it was getting closer!

Then, as suddenly as the horrific sound had begun, it stopped.

Nellie cautiously opened her eyes.

She was no longer in the dark, basement corridor. Now she knelt before a mirror, in another place. It was the large, ornate, gold mirror from the asylum entryway. She stared, mouth agape, at her reflection. It rippled. Her face began to pull and stretch, her body following suit by pinching and expanding, warping and distorting. As she watched, the reflection warped and twisted faster and faster until it fluttered at impossible speed.

Out of the darkness behind Nellie's fluctuating reflection, emerged the shadowed figure of a girl. Nellie could not see her face, but recognized the arms hanging lifelessly at her sides. Her tangled, dirt-encrusted hair could just be made out against the blackness of the shadows.

Nellie sat frozen in fear, unable to move.

"Wake up ...." The dry, raspy voice echoed around Nellie.

CHAPTER 9

Nellie awoke screaming. Powerful torrents of cold water flooded over her face and body, sending her into shock. She coughed and spluttered, desperately trying to wipe the water out of her face while gasping for breath. Even though her waterlogged eyes were still blurry, Nellie could make out that she was now naked, in a damp cement room, with pipes in the wall above her and a gurgling drain in the center of the floor. She wasn't alone.

Two figures in bulky suits strode toward her, holding poles with broom-like extensions on the ends. Their faces hidden behind their opaque-windowed face plates and square hoods that covered all distinguishing features. Was this really happening? Nellie scrambled backward on the wet, cement floor and slipped. The ominous figures approached, holding their "brooms" toward her.

"Get up," came a muffled voice. The masked figure jabbed at her with the strange scrubber. A tinny speaker in the ceiling projected another hard-to-discern voice: "Lift your arms up." Nellie looked from the speaker back to the figures and lifted her arms. The suited orderlies stood on either side and scrubbed her with the harsh bristles, chaffing her soft, pale skin until it was red and raw all over. The substance they scrubbed with smelled of lye. They left no part of her untouched, no crevice unscrubbed.

To add insult to injury, one orderly grabbed a hose attached to a spigot, cranked the handle, and hosed Nellie down like an unwanted dog on the lawn. She held her hands up to shield her face from the stinging blasts of water.

Finally, the tortuous cleansing ended and the orderlies left the room, slamming the door behind them.

Naked, shivering, and alone, Nellie sank to the floor and wept.

Nurse Ball rapped sharply twice on Dr. Braun's office door. "Enter," came his reply. She swept the door open and stepped through to find Dr. Braun reviewing medical files. The light from the window lit up the page in his hand, and she recognized it as the Recommendation for Referral by the bloody hand print that the sunlight silhouetted from the other side. Dr. Braun scowled at the page.

"Something wrong, doctor?"

"This Nellie Bly character intrigues me. She doesn't fit the profile of the other inmates. She's different."

Nurse Ball shrugged. "We do have all manner of patients here. Some need less support than others."

He peered over the top of the page, through his thick spectacles. "She has no relatives listed. She is a self-check-in. Yesterday, she mentioned that she wanted to go home to her relatives. Nothing adds up — a most unusual case."

Nurse Ball reflected on his statement, for a moment, and then nodded. "She strikes me as a person who doesn't seem to have any problem ... except, perhaps, with authority." The doctor held the page with the bloody handprint toward her and nodded.

Handing the referral and file back to Nurse Ball, he added, "Find out anything you can for me. I want to know everything about this Nellie Bly."

Faintly, Nellie wondered if this wasn't what the beginning stages of hypothermia felt like. She hugged her knees and noticed that her toenails and fingers had transformed from pink to a deep purple-blue. She was also certain that the fact that her body was no longer trembling, combined with the compelling urge to sleep were, in all likelihood, dangerous signs of her impending end. She let her eyes close, and the incoming wave of exhaustion began to carry her toward the promise of blissful peace.

Nellie …. The soft whisper of her name brought her back to consciousness. She had to force her eyelids to part and expose light to her blurry eyes. The dark, shadowy corner across the room seemed to move. "Get up!" The tinny speaker over her head sounded, and her sluggish system responded by jolting her with a fresh shot of adrenaline. She gasped, and her eyes opened wide. The shadows in the corner lightened.

"Time to get dressed."

The orderlies, in their bulky alien suits, reappeared through the door, bringing a gust of biting, cold air across her damp, blue skin. They pulled her to her feet, her numb feet painfully slapping against the frigid, wet cement, causing waves of prickling pain as circulation returned. When she raised her head again, to surmise her new surroundings, she found herself in a new room, empty save for two metal stools and a cot. The iron and brick walls were dark. The only light of the room came from a small slit of a window that was set too high for her to see out. In the wall to her right, there was another window-like hole, but this one was made of thick, opaque plastic that could not be seen through from inside the room.

"Put this on." The masked technician held out a dry, gray dress. She snatched it quickly from his gloved hand, and dropped it over her head and onto her shivering frame. Thin though it was, it was all that stood between her and pneumonia.

A bottle thunked down on one of the metal stools. "What's that for?" Nellie pointed.

"The doctor requires a sample of urine," replied a muffled voice, from somewhere inside the suit.

"What for?"

Wordlessly, the orderlies turned and exited, shutting the reinforced steel door tightly and engaging the lock.

"Hey! You can't do this!" Nellie pounded on the locked door with her fist and immediately regretted it. The pricking nerves of her still cold hand exploded with pain that shot through her arm and into her shoulder.

She returned to one of the metal stools and sat, cradling her throbbing hand. The heat of her boiling anger was enough to warm her whole body from within. She inwardly composed the next piece of her exposé.

"The water was ice-cold, and I again began to protest. How useless it all was! The orderlies began to scrub me. I can find no other word that will express it but scrubbing. With long, scratchy brushes, they took some soft soap and rubbed it all over me, even all over my face and my hair. I was, at last, past seeing or speaking. My teeth chattered and my limbs were goose-fleshed and blue with cold. Suddenly I was doused with buckets' worth of water — ice-cold water, from hoses — into my eyes, my ears, my nose and my mouth. I think I experienced some of the sensations of a drowning person as they dragged me, gasping, shivering, and quaking to my new home; a dark, stone box. For once I did look insane. They put me, dripping wet, into a gray, cotton flannel slip."

The door to the small room opened again, and this time it was a masked technician in a less bulky head-to-

toe uniform. He pulled the second stool over, next to Nellie and sat down to take her arm.

"What now?" she pulled her arm out of his grasp.

"We need blood." He pulled her arm back toward him with the tolerance of someone who had lived this scenario of resistance a hundred times over.

"Why?"

The hypodermic needle pierced her arm and filled with crimson.

"Protocol."

The needle withdrew in silence. The gray floor gained color as it met with spatters of Nellie's blood. The technician pressed on the needle-stick site for a few moments, to stop the blood, and then left with his vials. The lock in the door engaged once more.

Shadows moved behind the opaque plastic window in the iron wall. *Ah, this must be an observation window. They can see me but I cannot see them.*

"Enjoying the view?" she called toward the faceless observers. She dragged a stool to the opposite wall, to sit in the little patch of sunlight provided by the miniscule window. Plopping down on the stool, she folded her sore arms, leaned against the wall, and closed her eyes. Damned if she would give them a show of any sort.

It was hard to tell how much time had passed. When Nellie opened her eyes again, the patch of sunlight she had moved to was nowhere to be seen. It must have been the sound of the door being opened that woke her. One of the stools had been removed, and Nurse Ball now entered the small room, holding a tray that held a paper cup. She extended the tray to Nellie.

"What is this for?"

"Something to help you sleep. You have a big day tomorrow."

"What happens tomorrow?" Nellie sat up.

"Dr. Braun starts your treatment. You'll be well before you know it."

"Treatment?" Nellie was aghast. "He hasn't even given me a proper evaluation yet!"

The calm demeanor with which Nurse Ball typically addressed the inmates was shaken only when authority was questioned. She had an uncanny ability to change from commanding to imposing with very little effort.

"You'll do well not to argue."

Nellie felt that the "with me" was very much implied as Nurse Ball stared fixedly down at her from her lofty height. Nellie picked up the little, paper cup and tipped its contents quickly back into her mouth.

"See?" she forced a smile and showed Nurse Ball the empty cup. "All gone."

"Let me see under your tongue." Nurse Ball put her hand gently under Nellie's chin and lifted her face up.

Damn.

Nellie quickly slid the pills out from under her tongue and swallowed, and then allowed Nurse Ball to verify that the medication had been ingested. Satisfied, Nurse Ball turned on her heel, snatched up the stool, and moved purposefully to the door.

"Wait …." Nellie called out and stopped her as she opened the heavy door. "Are patients allowed to have any writing materials? Something? Anything?"

Nurse Ball's face softened. "I can bring crayons and a piece of paper later. You can use it to do something constructive. Creativity is always encouraged. G'night."

The heavy door shut with a clank. The lock engaged with what was becoming a familiar "snick".

As Nurse Ball's footsteps moved off into the distance, Nellie fell to the floor and stuck her fingers down her throat. She retched up the white pills, now partially dissolved. The liquid mixture of bile and drug trailed toward the drain in the middle of the floor.

Let it take its effect elsewhere.

They had only just begun to dissolve; perhaps she had gotten rid of them in time. She did her best to use her feet to smear the small puddle down the drain and remove the evidence. She was alone again, this time with only a rock-hard cot and a flat pillow. She collapsed onto the cot and pulled her knees up toward her chin.

"I could not sleep, so I lay in bed, picturing to myself the horrors that would ensue should a fire break out in the asylum. Every door is locked separately, and the windows are too small and too high making escape impossible. There are countless patients here. It is impossible to get out unless these doors are unlocked. A fire is not improbable, but one of the most likely occurrences. Should the building burn, the jailers or nurses would never think of releasing their crazy patients. This I can prove later when I come to tell of their cruel treatment of the poor things entrusted to their care. As I say, in case of fire, not a dozen women could escape. All would be left to roast to death. Even if the nurses were kind, which they are not, it would require more presence of mind than women of their class possess to risk the flames, and their own lives, while they unlocked the hundred doors for the insane prisoners. Unless there is a change, there will someday be a tale of horror never equaled."

She would have to find a way to preserve these words with the paper and crayon that Nurse Ball had promised.

But what value should I place in promises made to the insane?

She glanced up again at the impossibly small window. Only then did the true horror of her situation strike Nellie.

No evaluation. Only medication. No communication. No one to be trusted. How will I ever leave this godforsaken place? My plan for redemption has become my undoing!

"Oh God!" she cried out to the darkness. Her hand flew to her mouth to stifle the hiccupping sounds of the hot tears that flowed into the pathetic excuse for a pillow beneath her.

The black key slipped into the keyhole and, with a quick turn, pushed the tumblers in place. The door opened quietly and Dr. Braun checked over his shoulder. He was alone. With that assurance, he slipped inside the door and locked it again from the inside.

He pressed the light switch and the white room was instantly bathed in dim yellowish light, revealing the older female patient on the gurney at the far end of the room. He strode to the bed and carefully inspected the IV drip.

Her silver hair pooled beneath her head. Her once white gown had yellowed with age. He lifted the arm where the needle had been inserted into a vein and was taped down firmly to her paper-thin skin. The skin itself was purple and mottled around the needle. Dr. Braun frowned.

"No signs of infection at least," he said through gritted teeth.

He dropped her hand to the bed where it lay limp and unresponsive. He lifted her eyelids and checked each eye carefully.

"No dilation yet." He scribbled his findings and stats on a clipboard which lay on the night table. "And still no change!" He threw the clipboard roughly to its resting place beside the bed.

Dr. Braun pulled a syringe from his coat pocket, uncapped it, and tapped the glass vial. With a small squeeze, he ejected a spurt of medication through the needle to remove any air bubbles and promptly injected it into the IV line.

"That should do the trick."

He stood over the patient, frowning. Her treatment might need to become more aggressive soon. On that thought, he turned on his heel, shut out the light, unlocked the door, and checked the hallway.

Still no one there. He slipped silently back out, as he always did, locked the door, and patted the keys in his pocket as he went about his business.

CHAPTER 10

R usted metal pipes creaked and groaned.

Nellie spun around. She must be dreaming again. The long corridor that lead off into darkness, the walls that dripped with orange and red rust...this had all happened before.

There on the floor were the scattered pages. Would the masked-rabbit appear again?

She picked up a few pages and examined them. These were different than before but were definitely drawn by the same hand.

Shadows In The Basement

This illustration was of a machine of some sort. In the corner of the page a machine sat, enveloped in vaporous clouds that extended outward to become veins and arteries. The veins and arteries, in turn, twisted outward and over a square of light in which figures were illuminated: a deformed, demonic creature with catlike features; a terrified rabbit. Most curiously, the rabbit appeared to have a slightly transparent reflection in the square of light. Terrifying and demented faces appeared in each segment of the picture, causing Nellie to look more intently into each sweep of charcoal and every detailed smudge.

It wasn't until she realized her head was aching that she blinked and looked down the corridor again. Further down the corridor she heard something creak.

Nellie took a step toward the sound, toward the darkness. Her movement was not without difficulty. She knew that she would not be able to leave this place until she ventured forth. Yet she also knew, with great certainty, that whatever awaited her at the end of the corridor would not be something she wanted to meet face to face. With each step she took, the darkness grew thicker. The walls dripped more. The air became thinner. With every step, her heart beat faster and her breathing became shallower. This was surely what it must be like to be in a tomb.

Something appeared in the darkness — a dim light at the end of the corridor. Seeing the light ahead, Nellie's step lengthened and her pace increased. Finally, she reached the end of the corridor, and found herself standing before a large, steel, vaulted door. She hoped this would be the way out.

The silence was overwhelming. Nellie spun suddenly and looked into the stretching corridor behind her, but there was nothing.

She turned back to the ominous door and leaned forward. It was covered in layers of dirt and grime. This place had long been forgotten. Something caught her attention. She carefully wiped at what looked to be a stenciled letter. There was an "E." She wiped harder, feeling for lines in the grit on the door. Now there was an "I." Her fingertip turned black as she scrubbed harder and harder. A "C" appeared next to the "I."

I C E

The bulb above her flickered. Nellie froze, her heart pounding in her chest. She slowly turned to look over her shoulder, and gasped. Darkness moved down the hall toward her, swallowing everything in its path. There was nowhere to run.

Nellie panicked, flattened against the dirty, cold metal door behind her. The darkness was approaching so quickly that she was sure it would swallow her in a few moments.

The dry, rasping voice screeched from somewhere just in front of her: "Did you really think you'd find truth here? You've been left behind to DIE! LIKE THE REST OF US!"

The shrill voice reached a fever pitch that rattled Nellie's ears and sent ice pouring through her veins and electricity down her spine. From out of the darkness, a figure reached for Nellie and tore at the front of her dress, yanking her forward into the darkness. Nellie's terror tore the scream from her throat; she couldn't breathe ... couldn't breathe as the darkness enveloped her and she was swallowed by blackness, pulled downward by a supernatural force that she couldn't escape.

Nellie sat bolt upright in bed, gasping for breath. She looked around — at the walls, the cot, the heavy door. The hint of orange in the tiny band of dark sky that was visible through the window told her it was almost sunrise. She was ineffably relieved to find herself in her room in the asylum.

She closed her eyes, took a deep breath, and hung her head. The terror slowly faded with each deep breath in and out. Nellie let her head hang limply and allowed her shoulders to droop. There. Calm. She opened her eyes.

Nellie cried out. Her hand shaking uncontrollably, she pulled her dress out before her. A dirty handprint stained the front of her dress. It was roughly the size of a child's. She looked down to the floor to make sure she really had thrown up the medication. There was the faint streak of chalky matter leading to the drain. Yet there *was* a child's handprint on her dress. Her own trembling palms were clean. She stared at them.

The door to the room swung open and a flash of light blinded her. "Nellie? Are you alright?" Nurse Ball swung her flashlight's beam out of Nellie's eyes and swept the room with it. Nellie squinted, unable to speak for a few moments.

"Just —— just a bad dream, I think." She saw some crayons and a piece of paper on the floor next to the cot. "Thank you," she added.

"Come on, Nellie. How very late it's getting!" urged the nurse.

Nellie blinked. "I'm late?"

"Yes, you shall be late if we don't leave now. It's time to make introductions. Let's go."

CHAPTER 11

D r. Braun's blackboard did not have even a small square free of clutter. Every inch of its surface contained written notes, maps, charts or newspaper clippings. The most recent newspaper headlines screamed "COGNOME THEORY" and "SATURATION CHAMBERS, A CURE FOR THE MIND."

Dr. Braun pulled the rolling blackboard forward and flipped it over to its other side. Here were his personal studies, the research he pursued in the wee hours of the night or behind a locked office door. This side of the blackboard featured a giant, detailed diagram of a brain. Next to this diagram hung the side and front identification photographs the court had taken of Nellie for her admittance paperwork. Dr. Braun returned to his desk and to the metal tray that held the carcass of his test subject, a white rabbit, splayed on its back. Forceps and hooks held the rabbit's flesh open. The incision was an angry red slash defiling the otherwise pristine white coat of the small animal. He used a scalpel to probe into its flesh and expose an organ.

"Most interesting," he murmured.

Nellie followed the inmates before her in a daze, a line of blank faces shuffling single file, step by step, out into the common room. Orderlies poked and prodded at the particularly sluggish patients to keep the line moving at an even pace.

"Get moving." Nurse Ball nudged a meandering inmate along in the proper direction.

Nellie realized, with a start, that she was passing in

front of the ornate, gold mirror. She quickly averted her eyes. Whether it was the fact that the mirror was a key factor in her nightmares, or perhaps something more, did not matter. She just knew that she did not want to test those dark waters right now.

"Nellie!" Dorothy shimmied out of her own single file line, which was approaching from another hallway, and flitted over to slip into line just behind Nellie.

Dr. Braun tapped lightly on Nurse Ball's arm. "Come with me."

Nurse Ball followed Dr. Braun outside to a path that led around the edge of the grounds safely out of earshot of the patients and staff.

"Nurse, have you found anything on Miss Bly yet?"

Checking first to make sure no one was near them, Nurse Ball nodded, "Yes. It looks like she was just fired from her job as a reporter for The New York Tribune. It would seem that her investigations upset some people with influence and they demanded that she be removed from her position."

"Investigations?" Dr. Braun looked up at her and adjusted his spectacles.

"She went in disguise to expose slave owners, sweat shops, child labor — you name it, she has done it. I would even venture a guess that we might be the target of her current investigation," Nurse Ball sniffed.

Trying to get her job back then, is it?" The doctor stiffened. After a moment's pause, he added, "I tested her urine sample on the rabbit. Dissection revealed changes to the rabbit's reproductive system."

Nurse Ball came to an alarmed halt. "She's pregnant?"

He shushed her and glanced about.

"So there has to be a father. A man in her life." Nurse Ball shook her head. "I found no records of her being married."

"You and I know that there are plenty of children born outside the institution of marriage. But it is important to know if there is … well, who the father is."

They began to walk again and, having nearly completed the circuit of the courtyard path, approached the entryway where staff and patients alike might overhear their private conversation.

"Follow normal hospital procedures with her until we find out more. Good day, nurse." Dr. Braun nodded to a white-clad passerby. He pulled the staff door open and held it for Nurse Ball. "We have to be careful with this one," he said under his breath.

Nurse Ball nodded and stepped inside with Dr. Braun following. She stopped in front of the large, antique mirror. "I hate that mirror. Brings back bad memories," she scowled.

"On the contrary, I would say that mirror saved us, don't you think?" countered the doctor. They each took a moment to reflect on the mirror itself, lost in the ornate scrollwork, the nearly perfect glass surface. The nurse's face softened, revealing signs of a neglected and buried pain, as the disturbing memories flooded back.

Dr. Braun watched her extend her index finger toward the center of the glass, and followed her gaze to the mirror's center. Only her troubled and lost expression, and his curious gaze, reflected back at them.

"Nurse Ball?" a female nurse called out. Nurse Ball visibly twitched, and quickly retracted her hand.

"Yes, Nurse Murphy?" she turned and disappeared down the hallway to find the staff member in need of assistance.

"David! Hello there!" Dr. Braun suddenly called out to a passing orderly, who stopped to greet the doctor. "You know what I could really use assistance with...." Dr. Braun's voice trailed away as the two proceeded together down the opposite corridor.

Nellie was content to find a chair, in front of a table, where she could sit and observe. Dorothy had wanted to cheer herself up with a walk outside, so this quiet time would be a good chance to get something done. Armed with crayons and paper, it was easy enough to look busy to those who needed to see it. To the untrained eye, Nellie's squiggles and wiggly lines would look like a child's attempt to imitate handwriting, but it was actually a clever trick she had picked up in school. "Pitman shorthand" it was called, and it was a method of being able to safely write down her thoughts. Only someone with similar training would be able to decipher it. Similar training and the ability to speak German. It had proved the perfect method for keeping her diary private and her thoughts secret and now served her well in her career as a journalist.

"Oh that's just lovely, Nell!" Nurse Johnson exclaimed, with an encouraging clap of her hands. "Is that the ocean?"

Nellie nodded with equally enthusiastic delight. "Oh thank you, why yes it is! And I shall draw in the scones and jam and piano just … there!" she stabbed at the corner of the page with her fingertip.

"How lovely!" the nurse genuinely beamed, her

dimples accentuating her round, red cheeks and twinkling brown eyes. She patted Nellie's shoulder and made her way to the next inmate on her rounds. Nellie decided that not everyone in this place was cruel. She continued to record her observations, which would translate from shorthand and German thusly:

We were compelled to get up at 5.30 o'clock, and at 7.15 we were told to collect in the hall. When we got into the dining-room at last, we found a bowl of cold tea, a slice of buttered bread and a saucer of oatmeal, with molasses on it, for each patient. I was hungry, but the food would not go down. I asked for unbuttered bread and was given it. I cannot tell you of any natural thing which is the same dirty, black color. It was hard, and in places nothing more than dried dough. I found a spider in my slice, so I did not eat it. I tried the oatmeal and molasses, but it was wretched, and so I endeavored, without much show of success, to choke down the tea.

Her stomach rumbled. Nellie realized that the smell of something from the kitchen was wafting into the room. "Come to the hall!" one of the cooks called out. Perhaps the lunch fare would offer something more palatable. She filed into the cafeteria with a multitude of others who each, robotically, found a place on one of the many long benches. Like the rest of this institution, the decrepit state of everything, from the peeling walls to the smell of mold on the long, pock-marked tables, made the boarders feel thoroughly unwelcome. Yet here they came, in droves, to sit beside one another, arms on the tables, and wait for the next step of the repetitive schedule that constituted each dreary day.

Kitchen staff systematically plunked down small, tin plates in front of each woman. "No dining ware, of course," Nellie observed. She watched the inmates, with their food before them, grab at their single, small, tough piece of cold, boiled meat or their small, and slightly rancid, boiled potato. When a plate landed in front of her, with her portion of gray protein and a yellow-green knob of potato, she sniffed at it. She had actually hoped to want to eat it, but it only made her gag. She smiled weakly at the hunched, elderly woman with wiry, gray hair next to her and nudged the lunch plate over to her. This patient was not so picky, gruffly grunting her thanks and then gnawing on the cold lump with her toothless gums. Nellie felt her throat close and a cold sweat prickling upon her brow. She excused herself from the bench.

"Get your hands off me!" cried a familiar and outraged voice. Nellie turned to see the girl with the ragged, blue bow hanging from her neglected, wild, red hair. She was, yet again, at the bottom of a pile of staff vigorously trying to pin the girl to the floor.

"You're all just a bunch of slaves!" her screed continued from somewhere on the floor amidst the scuffling and grunting of Nurse Ball and her attending orderlies.

Then the girl made her worst mistake yet. Nellie watched, wide-eyed, as the redhead grabbed a fistful of Nurse Ball's hair and yanked. The girl dismantled the perfect bun that adorned Nurse Ball's head causing hair pins to fall to the floor with soft, high-pitched tinks. The look in Nurse Ball's eyes gave Nellie a chill. In that moment that the girl yanked on the roots of Nurse Ball's hair, Nellie saw the large whites of the Head Nurse's eyes and she observed the pinpoint rage with which she locked eyes with the girl. The effect was instantaneous; the girl's eyes grew saucer-like and her hand dropped.

"Take Wendy to her room. This instant." The cold words were nearly hissed through solidly clenched teeth, the intensity with which she emphasized the "t" resembling a disapproving "tsk" from a headmaster.

The staff wasted no time in collecting the girl. Frightened into submission by the Head Nurse's stare, the girl offered no more resistance, compliantly getting to her feet and moving as fast as she could out of Nurse Ball's reach. And while no one knew for sure what fate awaited young Wendy, everyone who could comprehend what just happened knew that they would not want to be in her place tonight. They all silently watched the group exit the dining hall and sweep around the corner.

Nellie sauntered to the spot where the scuffle had taken place and swept the freed hairpins from the grimy floor and into her pocket. She smiled and headed for the common room. Dorothy sat on the floor, with her legs tucked underneath her, braiding one side of her hair. She looked up and grinned to see her companion approach.

"Well you certainly look better today. Is everything ok?" she inquired.

"Just grand," Nellie smiled. She sat beside Dorothy to help with her other braid.

With the sun set and the moon on its ascent, the asylum began the nightly lockdown routine. Nellie and Dorothy were sent to shuffle, single-file, with their wing-mates back to their rooms for the night. With each patient in her room, staff walked the halls, unlocking and locking the outside door bolts to assure that they were fully engaged.

Nellie lay on her cold hard cot and listened as banks of lights were shut down by switches somewhere outside her room. The lights went out. Thankfully the minuscule square of moonlight from her room's thin window provided just enough light. She got up from the cot, pulled a hairpin from her pocket and got to work on the door lock.

Tap, tap, tap, tap.

Whatever this sound was, it echoed in the hall. It was getting steadily closer and louder. She realized that it was coming toward her door. Nellie flattened herself against the wall next to her door and held her breath.

A small shadow blocked the scant bit of light that glimmered from under her door. Nellie bit her lip and waited, her last breath held securely in her chest.

After what felt like an eternity, the shadow dashed away. She exhaled, and, as the air escaped from its prison it carried with it some her tension and fear. With a steady hand, she returned to working at the lock.

CLICK!

"Another win for the intrepid reporter!" Nellie thought, gleefully. The heavy door to her room swung open with a groan.

Nellie froze. The hair on her arms stood up. Her mouth went dry. She was not alone in her solitary confinement.

A gurgling, wheezing sound approached from the shadows behind her. "Youuuuu — you killed the rabbit," a grating voice rattled.

Nellie spun around. There was the girl from her nightmares. Her blond dirty, tangled hair hung limply in her face, and down over her torn, blood-spattered dress. But now, in the faint light cast from the doorway, Nellie saw her eyes. They were red. And, suddenly, those terrifying eyes widened with rage.

"THE RABBIT DIED BECAUSE OF YOU!"

The horrid apparition flew from the shadows, toward Nellie, its arms outstretched to capture her in it's decaying grip. Her fury pulled her along the floor straight to Nellie. With a furious shriek, the girl's mouth came at Nellie's face, its open mouth a black hole lined with decaying teeth and rotting flesh.

Nellie fell backward and scrambled, as fast she could, into the hall. She jumped to her feet and flattened herself against the wall opposite her door. Her heart in her mouth, she watched everything around her, wild-eyed.

She listened, trying to hear above the pounding in her ears and her own ragged breathing. Then … nothing.

Nellie leaned toward the door of her room. It was completely empty. Up and down the hallway — empty. There was nothing to hear except intermittent wails from the other floors and loud snores from the adjacent rooms. Nellie held her head in her hands and took several deep breaths. Was this vision a result of the medication? Or was she somehow becoming a victim of her environment? The soft step of a night nurse echoed from somewhere near the end of the hall causing Nellie to snap to attention. She didn't have time for hallucinations. She couldn't miss this opportunity. She shut her unlocked door and moved with swift, quiet strides down the hall, careful to stay close to the walls and in the shadows.

It wasn't long before she arrived at Dr. Braun's office and, pulling a hairpin from her pocket, made quick work of its lock. With the door open, she stepped inside. The large window next to his desk allowed the moonlight to bathe the office in soft, white light that shone through some of the specimen jars, giving them an eerie glow. Nellie wasted no time. She quickly rifled through the stacks of documentation that were scattered about on the counters and on his desk. Medical records here, patient progression notes there. Nothing of use would likely be lying out in the open. She turned and scanned the office for a prime location to contain more secret documentation. Then she spied it: the file cabinet. She moved past the desk and chair, crossing the office to the cabinet. She gave the handle a sharp tug and found it locked, and, unfortunately, locked by something more complicated than her hairpin skills could handle. She put her hands on her hips and looked around the room again from this new perspective.

There was a blackboard with a sheet over it. That was as good a place to look as any. Nellie grasped the sheet and flipped the corner up so she could take in the blackboard's contents. It was not unlike trying to decipher her own shorthand, in that it was a series of complicated formulas and unusual drawings. But this was something she could work on later. She pulled a fresh sheet of paper and a crayon from her pocket and sketched out some of the most prominent formulas and theorems. "What are you trying to do, Doctor?" she murmured. Her hand came to a sudden halt when her eyes fell on the title at the bottom of the blackboard:

PROJECT : ALICE

Nellie left the room exactly as she had found it and, with the sketches safely in her pocket, locked the door and skittered along the halls back to her room. She slipped through the door to her cell and, after a thorough review of the shadows and the space beneath her cot, she closed the door sealing herself inside. Her new crayon-sketched findings would need to be hidden somewhere. These couldn't be explained away as an ocean-view, particularly if the doctor himself were to find them. The cot offered no refuge for her treasures; papers would be easily discovered there with the most basic inspection. The legs weren't hollow, so that would not do either.

She inspected the bricks in the wall of the window. Mortar crumbled away here and there, perhaps she could find a loose brick? Nellie patiently felt along each row of bricks, pushing and prying at each one in turn. She gently pushed her cot out of the way and continued until — ah-ha! — one brick in particular seemed a bit looser than the rest. Carefully, she pulled and pried at one side until the end began to give. With a begrudging scrape, the brick came out and Nellie stuffed her folded page into the hole in the base of the wall behind her cot.

She stopped as her fingertips brushed something cold and metallic in the space behind the bricks. Gently, she picked up a delicate strand with something attached, and held it up to the moonlight. A gold locket, tarnished with age and dirt, dangled from her fingers. She quickly replaced the brick, slid the cot back against the wall and scrambled atop her bed. Standing on the cot so that she could use the moonlight from the window for a closer look, she placed the locket in the palm of her hand and examined the design on the front. It was an odd design comprised of what appeared to be caterpillars. She polished the locket on her shift and looked again — yes, caterpillars.

"What in the world?" she muttered.

She used the edge of her thumbnail to delicately pop the tiny closure on the locket and swing its small door open. Inside, instead of a photograph, solid perfume, paper, strand of hair, or other expected article of remembrance or affection, Nellie found instead a small pile of powder. She touched it. It was soft and fine, like talcum powder, but if it was talcum powder, she could not smell it. Perhaps the talc was so aged, its perfume had dulled. She brought the powder closer, to give it a whiff.

"Ugh!" she recoiled at the foul scent and snapped

the offensive locket shut. Instantly, she felt sick to her stomach. What had she just ingested? Her head began to reel, and she clutched at her stomach … the pain was horrid!

Before she could call for help, her eyes fluttered and she collapsed on her cot, unconscious.

Somewhere in the basement of Bedlam Asylum, pipes lined the walls and groaned, dripping orange and red with moist rust. Down at the end of the long, dark corridor, a single light bulb barely illuminated an old, heavy, dirt-encrusted vault door.

The bulb began to flicker.

And, from somewhere behind the vault door, a voice emanated, singing softly, rattling like musty air passing over dusty, decaying vocal chords:

Doctor locked me behind a great door:

Doctor left me forever more.

And all of his nurses and all of his men,

Won't be able to put Doctor together again.

Doctor put a hole in my head:

Doctor, can't wait until you're dead.

And all of your nurses and all of your men,

Won't be able to put you together again.

CHAPTER 12

Aface loomed directly over hers, its wide eyes gaping. Nellie awoke with a squawk and jerked back on her cot.

"Oh!" Dorothy stood upright. "I'm sorry, Nellie, I didn't mean to startle you!"

"Dorothy?" Nellie said with closed eyes, her hand over her thumping heart. Her splitting headache made her eyes too blurry to trust. "Where am I?"

"We're in your room." Dorothy kneeled next to her and took her hand.

"What? How did you get in here?"

"It's free time. Two o'clock. I was worried when you didn't come out for breakfast or dinner. It'll be supper before you know it. Are you okay?"

"Yeah, I think so. Just had a bad dream." Nellie pulled herself up into a sitting position on her cot. "Let's find somewhere to go sit. I've been in this room long enough."

Instead of returning to the main common area, Nellie and Dorothy passed by the bustling, large room in favor of finding new places to explore. They wandered down the hall of the wing that held Dorothy's room and, at the other end of the long, green hall, found a smaller and older common room.

This room was devoid of life in every way. It definitely had the same elements of neglect as everything else in the establishment, the cracks in the wall and peeling plaster, dingy floors, and over-used chairs and tables from yesteryear. It held a few of the same asylum-safe items that could be found in the main common room: a checker board, decks of playing cards, old books. One table even featured a dusty chess board with the white army arranged on one side and the red on the other. But this room had one unusual addition to the decay: the walls had a charred appearance, and the faint smell of burnt paper hung in the still air.

Had there been a fire at Bedlam? Nellie thought back to her worries about what might happen in this place if all of the patients had to quickly make an escape to avoid disaster. Bedlam offered no safety to those locked within its walls if a fire broke out. If this room was evidence that something nefarious had transpired, Nellie would get to the bottom of it.

But first, she needed to rest. Dorothy could see that Nellie was pale and weary, and so she found a chair for her. Nellie smiled gratefully and went to sit, touching Dorothy's hand in thanks.

"Oh, look," Nellie stopped halfway to the chair and pointed to a stuffed child's toy that had fallen from a side table. She took a few steps and bent to pick up the forgotten teddy bear. It was an odd thing to find in Bedlam, considering that even Dorothy, a girl in her teens, was supposedly too young to be admitted into Bedlam. Perhaps it had once belonged to a patient who fancied herself childlike. Nellie's fingertips touched the soft down of the tattered, honey-brown bear.

"Those are MINE!" the child's voice rang out, brimming with defiance. "I don't like it when people take things that belong to me!" The room around Nellie had changed. She stood up, swimming in a sea of confusion. The large, old room was now significantly smaller and appeared to be more like a typical inmate's cell. She looked about her and could not see Dorothy in this new place that now contained only a cot and the side table with the red and white chess set. Suddenly, a rush of inmates pushed and shoved their way through the door and into the room. They swarmed in, knocking Nellie over onto the floor and searching high and low for something. From behind Nellie, the voice continued, accompanied by the stamp of a small foot. "What is she doing here? Get her out. GET HER OUT!"

"Nellie?" Dorothy's far-off voice floated into Nellie's ear.

Nellie blinked. She was back in the old common room with Dorothy, who held her arm and searched her face for any sign that she could comprehend where she was.

"Are you okay? Talk to me, Nell!"

Nellie opened her mouth to speak, but another voice interrupted.

"I warned you about Alice. Now she's in your head. And she won't get out ...."

Both Nellie and Dorothy turned to the source of the voice. In the doorway stood Wendy, her shock of fiery, unkempt hair a direct contrast to her current predicament. She stood before them confined to a straightjacket. Her pink lips were outlined with crusty, chalky drool.

There's that medication. Nurse Ball's answer to quieting the unruly.

Wendy smiled as she rocked back and forth.

"I told you so, I told you so ..." she said pointedly to Nellie before turning away. Weaving, she wandered away down the hall, singing loudly:

Doctor wanted into her dreams,

Alice can't wait to hear your screams.

And all of your nurses and all of your men,

Won't be able to put you together again.

Wendy's off-key notes echoed back to them. To Nellie's surprise, it was Dorothy who spoke next.

"She's right, you know. Let's not put ourselves anywhere near Alice."

"Dorothy, what do you know about Alice?"

"Only that I can feel her. Same as you." Dorothy's face was pale as she looked away from Nellie. Nellie shook her head.

"No Dorothy. It's those pills. The pills they make us take." She gently turned Dorothy's face back toward hers. "They are causing us all to hallucinate."

Dorothy pulled away. "Alice is NOT a hallucination."

Again, Nellie was taken aback by Dorothy's unexpected intensity. She tried a different tack. "Look, I know I'm not crazy. But if you stay here long enough, this place will drive anyone insane."

"Uncle Henry and Aunt Em say it will get me better," Dorothy murmured.

"I wouldn't count on it. We need to get out."

Nellie thought for a moment. She suddenly sat straight up. "Is there a telephone? My editor can get us out. We need a telephone!"

"There are some in the hallway, down there. But we're not allowed —"

Nellie put her hand on Dorothy's arm. "Take me there. Now."

Dorothy peeked around the corner and watched for a good minute or two. When she was absolutely sure no one was coming, she slipped around the corner, pulling Nellie behind her.

"I found them yesterday while you were still asleep in your room," she whispered. "I wanted to try using one, but Nurse Murphy stopped me and told me we're not allowed to go near them until we earn it."

A row of dilapidated phone booths lined the far wall. Nellie's heart leapt with hope. She had been less than a week in the institution, but without any way to communicate to the outside world, and with all of the strange goings-on, she had had quite enough of being incarcerated. This was her chance to save herself, Dorothy, and, with the publication of her exposé, perhaps hundreds of lost souls.

Nellie snatched up the receiver of the first phone and waited for the operator to come on the line. Nothing happened. "This one's dead."

"I'll keep a lookout. Go ahead and try the rest!" Dorothy motioned her toward the phones and took up her post, keeping an eye out.

"This one, too." Nellie quickly dropped the receiver back into place and moved to the next. The hope that had, just moments before, practically lifted her across the floor was now rapidly dwindling as she realized that this, like everything else in Bedlam, was most likely just a façade. She wondered if Dr. Braun wasn't just a man behind a big, red curtain labeled "Bedlam Asylum."

Nellie worked her way through each telephone with the same result. There were only a couple left to try.

"They're all broken!" Nellie whispered, with despair.

Dorothy looked over her shoulder to Nellie, her face awash with anxiety. Nellie reached for another telephone receiver, closed her eyes and listened. "Hello, how may I direct your call?" the operator's nasal voice piped through the receiver.

"Oh thank God!" Nellie nearly sobbed with relief. Dorothy flashed her a big grin and returned to her hall monitoring. "I need an outside line to Algonquian 42, please," Nellie said in low tones, cupping her hand over her mouth.

"I'm sorry, miss, can you please repeat that?" the voice on the other end replied.

At the nurse's station, the telephone operator sat before a switchboard panel containing a dizzying array of plugs, bells, sockets, circuits, and wires. She tapped her headset and frowned, concentrating her listening efforts on each word spoken on the other end of the line. She pressed her headset against her ear. "You need an outside line?"

Nurse Ball, who stood on the other side of the counter, stopped organizing her paperwork and whisked around the counter. The operator put her hand over the receiver. "Someone is asking for an outside line but it isn't the doctor or any of the staff. This woman isn't using any of the code words."

"Where is the call coming from?" the nurse fired the question at the operator.

"The Fantasyland Wing, ma'am."

"Keep her on the line. I'll take care of it," Nurse Ball said and swept back around the counter and down the hall. Her shoes made the distinct clomping sound that the rest of the staff recognized as Nurse Ball on a mission. The staff and patients had two choices in that situation; either to try to keep up with her or to get the hell out of her way. In this case, the patients who saw her striding their way, skirt swinging out behind her, made efforts to side step as hastily as their clumsy feet would allow.

Nurse Ball wordlessly motioned to a group of orderlies to follow her.

The Operator pulled her hand away from the headset receiver.

"I'm sorry, ma'am. That exchange does not exist," came the voice from the other end of the line.

Nellie could have spit nails. This was not the time for her salvation to rest on the shoulders of the insipidly stupid. "What do you mean it doesn't exist? It DOES exist. It's the offices of the New York Tribune!"

"I show no such listing, ma'am."

Her heart sank like a stone. Even worse, the line began to snap and pop with static.

Dorothy gasped, spun around and tugged at Nellie's sleeve. "We have to go now, Nell. Really and truly!"

"Miss, I don't know who you are, but please listen to me," panic crept into Nellie's voice. "This is an emergency. I absolutely have to reach someone to let them know where I am. I need to speak to the Editorial Department at the New York Tribune newspaper. It really is a matter of life and death!"

"Are you sure you don't want to try a different exchange?" the nasal-toned operator said, with absolutely no emotion.

"LISTEN to me! I NEED to SPEAK to my EDITOR!" Nellie shouted into the receiver. The sound on the other end was that of the operator speaking, but it was masked behind crackling and popping. "Hello? Are you there?" Nellie stomped her foot. The receiver hissed in her ear like someone turning up the volume on a static-filled radio. Nellie pressed the receiver to her ear, making the greatest of efforts to make out what was happening on the other end of the telephone.

Barely audible behind the static and hissing, Nellie listened to the sound of a Victrola playing a warbling tune. She pulled the receiver away from her ear and looked at it. Was this happening, or was this another hallucination?

"Hello?" A voice she could not place as female or male spoke so softly that she could barely discern the words. " ... do not go ..."

"We need you ..." said another voice, this one deep and scratchy. " ... to keep Dorothy ...." a raspy, high-pitched voice finished.

Nellie's heart began thumping uncontrollably. She glanced over her shoulder to the young girl in braids who was scanning up and down the halls.

"Who is this?" she whispered.

Meowwwwww .... A tomcat's long, irritated howl crawled through the receiver and into her ear, raising the hair on the back of her neck.

"We're all mad here," another voice whispered.

The clomping sound was rapidly growing louder in the hallway.

"Nell!" Dorothy pulled on Nellie's arm.

The receiver was abruptly yanked from her hand and slammed back into the telephone's cradle. Nellie spun around and came nose to nose with Nurse Ball. A team of orderlies formed a wall behind her. Dorothy had backed up against the wall as if wanting to blend into it.

"Patients must earn telephone privileges, Miss Bly. Until then, a telephone call is strictly off limits." Nurse Ball stood upright and peered down her nose at Nellie, almost daring her to say something back.

Nellie's eyes narrowed. She stood up to her full height. She wasn't as tall as Nurse Ball, but she had had it with her "big and imposing" act. She wanted to make it clear that it didn't work on her anymore.

Nellie made herself as big as possible and leaned in to Nurse Ball. "You have no right to keep us isolated like this!"

It was Nurse Ball's turn to lean in. "We have rules here, Miss Bly. And you are to obey them or we will be forced to —"

"To what? Send me home?" Nellie interjected.

"To REPRIMAND you," Nurse Ball glowered. "Let me remind you that you signed a piece of paper, which has been filed with the court. That piece of paper says that we can keep you here as long as we see fit. And right now, Miss Bly, it looks like it may be a LONG time before we ever revisit the idea of your being well enough to reenter society."

Her fingertips came to rest on one of the syringes hanging from her belt. Nellie stared back at her with hate-filled eyes, clamping her lips shut.

Nurse Ball smirked. "Go ahead. Say one more word."

Dorothy cowered against the wall, away from the impending fray, biting her lip so hard that a drop of blood welled up on her lower-lip. "Nellie, no!" she whispered.

Nellie smirked up at the tall nurse, arms folded defiantly on her chest.

"Word."

"Right." Nurse Ball pulled the syringe from her belt, and the orderlies surrounding her leapt forward to grab Nellie and hold her still.

"Oh, Nellie!" Dorothy's eyes filled with tears as she

helplessly watched Nurse Ball jab the syringe into Nellie's right arm and her form crumple immediately into the arms of the men in white.

"I recommend you choose better friends, Miss Gale. This one is a bad influence." Nurse Ball wiped the needle of the empty syringe on her sleeve and deposited it back onto her belt.

"Yes, ma'am," Dorothy replied softly, her lower lip quivering and her eyes filling with tears.

Nurse Ball lifted Dorothy's chin to look her in the eyes. "Now you get out of here before I put you in seclusion too."

Dorothy said nothing and scrambled off down the hall toward the common room, tears flowing freely. She stopped to look back over her shoulder searching for Nellie, but they had taken her in a different direction. Crushed, Dorothy turned back, biting her lip again.

As she entered the common room, she felt a warm trickle run down her chin. She wiped her finger over the spot and realized, as she pulled it away covered in red, that her lip was bleeding. She had anxiously bitten her lip deeply enough that it had split. With nothing else to clean her face, she used the inside edge of neck of her dress.

As she cleaned her face, she became aware that it was deathly quiet. Dorothy looked up from the neck of her dress to find that every inmate in the common room now stood facing her and staring, mouths agape. Each set of eyes stared at her as if she were a murderer caught red-handed.

Dr. Braun and his orderlies arrived in the common room from the opposite entrance. Surmising what might be about to happen, David moved to intervene.

Dr. Braun put his hand on David's arm and whispered, "Wait. Let's observe."

Dorothy took a step backward, looking from inmate to inmate. They all just stared at her, arms hanging limply at their sides.

"Alice warned us about you," a patient said, pointing to Dorothy and stepping toward her.

Dorothy took another step back.

"You are dangerous," another intoned, also moving toward her. They each began to step toward the wide-eyed girl in braids.

"You must be stopped," said a bug-eyed woman. She raised her arms and lunged toward Dorothy. Before she could get away, several inmates had Dorothy's arms, and they grabbed and scratched at her relentlessly.

"No!" she cried out, "Let go of me!"

Dorothy yanked her arm forcefully out of the grasp of the bug-eyed woman. The woman's long, sharp nails rent Dorothy's skin as she pulled away, and blood welled up into the scratches. Other inmates grabbed at both of Dorothy's arms and pushed in, mobbing the young girl. She was being crushed by a pack of lunatics, and no one would come to her aid.

Panic bubbled up from her stomach and into her chest like a spark bursting into flame. "GET AWAY FROM ME!" she screamed and, with a mighty effort, crossed her arms in front of her face.

The inmates flew backward through the air away from Dorothy. Some smashed against and slid down the wall, loosening bits of plaster as they went. Others landed in the center of the room, smashing through tables and chairs. Some moaned and nursed their injuries while others cried and wailed.

"It's amazing ..." Dr. Braun breathed, the beginnings of a smile playing at the corners of his mouth. The orderlies left his side to rush to the aid of the wounded. David knelt beside Dorothy, who lay curled in a fetal ball on the floor, weeping and shuddering. She was repeating the same thing over and over to herself.

"What are you saying?" he put his hand gently on her shoulder.

" ... not again ... not again ..." Dorothy kept whispering, holding her knees to her chest and keeping her eyes squeezed shut.

"She's just like Alice." Dr. Braun grinned.

The keyhole clicked to the door on the sixth floor. When the door swung open, Dr. Braun hurriedly wheeled a cart into the room and locked the door behind him once more.

He hit the switch and the light bulb cast sickly yellow light on the woman's pale face. She lay on her pillow, utterly still, just as she always had.

"We're going to try a different method today," he said and parked the cart alongside the gurney. Dr. Braun slid a bite-down into the woman's mouth and secured her mouth shut.

He pulled the cart's wooden box closer to the woman's bed and cranked the handle until the box hummed. Dr. Braun swiped up a dab of jelly onto his fingertip and touched some to either side of her head.

He flipped the box lid open and removed two wood handled metal paddles. With a flip of a switch, the device's needle jumped to the right and into the red zone.

"Fully charged," Dr. Braun muttered. Holding the small paddles carefully, he brought them to the woman's temples and touched them to her skin.

The smell of ozone wafted upward as the current traveled through the woman's brain. Her eyes danced beneath their lids and her body stiffened with the current. He counted out loud, "1…2…3…4…5…and release."

He removed the paddles. She fell back to the mattress. He quickly lifted her eyelids, checking the dilation of her eyes. No response came. He put his stethoscope to her chest and listened. Her heart rate remained slow and steady. Her breathing was unchanged. The only notable difference with the woman was that her temples were now red and burnt.

"DAMN IT!" he bellowed.

His anger boiled over and he lashed out. Dr. Braun upset the entire cart, spilling its contents across the floor.

CHAPTER 13

N ellie found herself standing in the long, dark corridor, in the stretch where the shadows were darkest and the musty air hung, still and thick. Something had changed since she had been there last. The shadows ... they were different somehow. She examined them more closely. What had changed? Were they lighter somehow?

One of the shadows moved.

Nellie's knees trembled and she took a step back against the wall. A young girl stepped out of the shadows, toward Nellie. But this girl, she was very little, with soft brown curls and a modest gray dress like

Nellie's. She smiled up at Nellie, revealing dimples beneath her rosy cheeks and large blue eyes.

"Are you ... Alice?"

The little girl shook her head and smiled, drawing a half circle in the dirt with her toe. Nellie watched her with trepidation. She was simply adorable, but that only added to the mystery. Not only did a little girl not belong in Bedlam, but why would she be in this dark corridor born of nightmares? Nellie cautiously knelt down to the small girl's eye level.

"Are you okay? What's your name?"

"My name is Rose." She pulled one of her ringlets out, spring-like, and watched it bounce back into place.

"Hello Rose. That sure is a pretty name." Nellie smiled and brushed a curl from the girl's forehead. Rose nodded bashfully, and grinned.

"What are you doing down here, Rose? Did you lose your mama?" Rose looked at her with big, blue eyes and shook her head. She pointed to the end of the hall where the dim light bulb cast a sickly, yellow light on the grimy vault door.

She brushed Nellie's cheek with her small soft fingers. "Please don't let the bad men hurt me."

Her words tore straight through Nellie like a knife through tissue paper, and she could not fathom why this feeling of sorrow was so profound. Tears cascaded down Nellie's cheeks and, more than anything, she needed to protect this little girl. She put her arms around the small shoulders and pulled her close. Beneath her fingers, the diaphanous feeling of Rose's dress disappeared, and Nellie's arms closed on nothingness.

She was gone.

Nellie knelt on the gray dirty floor and wept with a depth of grief she had never known before, yet couldn't understand why.

CHAPTER 14

Nurse Ball glided into Dr. Braun's office to find him scribbling away with chalk, adding to his cluttered blackboard. She silently crossed over to the window and threw open the dusty shutters, instantly flooding the room with sunlight.

"Gah!" he threw his arm across his squinting eyes. "I didn't ask for more light, Nurse!" He whipped a handkerchief from his pocket and proceeded to sneeze repeatedly.

"You didn't request fresh air either, Doctor, but this office is still in great need of it," she said, sliding the stiff window upward. A small butterfly passed briefly between the iron bars of the window, carried by the fresh breeze on a sporadic flight path that led back out into the courtyard.

"Anyway, that Nellie Bly is turning out to be quite a … what are you doing?" Nurse Ball warily eyed the series of new theorems scrawled across the blackboard that she felt contained his most questionable work.

Tacked to the blackboard was what appeared to be a new photograph, which the breeze was keeping flipped upward and out of view. Dr. Braun spun toward Nurse Ball, beaming. This alone was cause for alarm. "I figured out the problem, Nurse Ball. All we needed was a control subject."

Nurse Ball could not take her eyes from the blackboard, watching for the moment when the breeze would relinquish control over that new paper.

"Doctor," she spoke carefully. "That is your research for Project Alice."

"Indeed!" he grinned. "And I've found another test subject!"

Nurse Ball stepped between the window and the blackboard, hands folded across her skirt. The photograph floated back down to settle against the blackboard.

"Dorothy Gale." Even as she spoke the name she had mostly expected, the shock brought on by the realization of the doctor's intentions washed over her. Her lips twitched.

After a few moments, she finally spoke again. "We can't possibly revive Project Alice. Not after what happened."

The doctor, known for neither warmth nor empathy, reached out to place his hand reassuringly on Nurse Ball's rigid arm.

"It will be different this time, Nurse, I assure you. She's far more manageable than Alice ever was."

Nurse Ball removed her arm from his grasp, eyes flashing. "You can't be serious! You are messing with powers that we don't —"

"They are not powers, Nurse Ball — merely physical manifestations from the minds of deluded young girls and their imaginary worlds."

He strode to his blackboard, flipped it over, and

picked up a piece of chalk. "Dorothy," he placed the chalk next to Dorothy's photograph, "shares the same peculiarities as Alice." He drew a line to the photograph of a beautiful young girl with long, silky, light hair and bright eyes. "They both exhibit physical links with their imaginary worlds."

"Doctor, even if you understood those links, how do you intend to control them?" He flipped the blackboard back over and jabbed the chalk at the photograph of Nellie.

"This time, we have the benefit of a control subject, Nurse Ball. A third person to act as a funnel, so to speak."

"Nellie Bly?" Nurse Ball's pained expression illustrated to Dr. Braun that this discussion would not soon be over.

Tap, tap, tap.

Nellie's eyes shot open. The last time she'd heard tapping coming her way, the results had been horrific. She craned her stiff neck to see the opaque window in the door. Someone was tapping a fingernail lightly against the glass.

"Nellie?" came the harsh whisper. "It's me, Dorothy!"

"I'm in here," Nellie replied, just loud enough to be heard through the door. The sound of the door swinging open with a creak was followed by a gasp. Dorothy was silent, overwhelmed with shock at seeing Nellie suspended by chains and pulleys six feet from the floor.

"It looks worse than it feels, Dorothy," she sighed. "I'm okay, just sore."

"Oh Nellie," wide-eyed Dorothy's fingertips hovered in front of her O-shaped mouth.

Nellie didn't want her to worry. "Dorothy, what are you doing here?" Her body swung gently back and forth from the chains, like a pendulum.

Dorothy held onto one of the chains with a firm hand and stilled the swaying. "That mean nurse told me not to talk to you anymore, but I wanted to make sure you're okay."

"I'm fine, really. I'm not worth you getting into trouble." Nellie watched the window above her, making sure none of the observers from the other side might suddenly appear.

"Oh don't say things like that," Dorothy's lower lip stuck out just a bit, as it usually did when she began to pout. "Nellie, they're putting me in a tank of some kind in just a couple hours. I'm scared."

Nellie tried, with great effort, to turn her head to look at Dorothy. "What tank?"

"They say it's part of my treatment."

"Dorothy, listen to me. They are NOT treatments, not at all. They are experiments. You absolutely must keep your mind focused. Don't take any pills that they give you. Spit them out if you must."

CLANK!

Dorothy whipped around to look out the doorway toward the loud sound. "I have to go now!"

"Dorothy, wait! When I get out of here, I promise, I'm taking you with me."

Dorothy paused for a moment, both hands worrying the end of a braid. She looked up with watery brown eyes to Nellie. "You promise?"

"I promise. I won't leave you behind." Dorothy smiled. In one swift movement, she stood up on her tip toes, kissed Nellie's cheek, and darted away out the door.

Nellie sighed. Clearly no one would be leaving Bedlam anytime soon if she couldn't find a way out of these restraints. She scrutinized each link in the solid chains that held her legs in place and followed them up to the pulley system that hung from the ceiling. With the shadows there, it was difficult to see how they were anchored.

She stared hard at the shadows. With a sickening feeling growing in the pit of her stomach, she watched the shadows move. They shifted, growing outward across the ceiling, like smoke pouring into the room. The black tendrils grew, scuttling down the chains that held Nellie suspended over the floor. Nellie thrashed her arms and legs, screaming and kicking, to no avail.

"HEEEEELLLPPPPP!!!!" she shrieked toward the open doorway.

The blackness coalesced directly over Nellie, a nimbus cloud just inches from her face. Tendrils stretched toward Nellie's shoulders, reaching for her skin. It was hair — long, tangled, dead, blond hair, pooling in circlets on Nellie's torso.

"SOMEBODY! ANYBODY!" Nellie's screams reached fever pitch, echoing down the halls outside. Red eyes emerged from the blackness over Nellie's face with the gurgling, wet sound of Alice's now all too familiar approach.

"You think you know your little friend?" the decaying face over Nellie's lilted, with a mocking grin. Cold, red viscera dripped from the maw down onto Nellie's skin.

"Be careful Nellie. Dorothy is more dangerous than she seems ...." The last word hissed through broken teeth.

Nellie squeezed her eyes shut. "Go away, go away, go away, go away," she muttered, convincing herself that this was yet another hallucination brought on by Nurse Ball's infamous syringe cocktails.

"Nellie Bly!" Nurse Ball clomped into the room followed by the sounds of several pairs of feet. "I think you've learned your lesson, wouldn't you say?"

Nellie cautiously opened one eye to look. No more Alice. She pressed her chin against her chest, looking for evidence. As she suspected, nothing.

Nurse Ball loosened the pulley's line that held Nellie's body aloft. The closer she was lowered to the floor, the more panic and tension flowed out of Nellie's body. As her body finally came into contact with the gurney, she had reached a level of calm in which she was thoroughly convinced that the apparition she had invented of Alice had a pattern of manifesting itself whenever Nellie felt stress or guilt regarding Dorothy. The orderlies removed the chains from the straps, leaving Nellie to relax on the gurney. They promptly exited the seclusion room.

Clinically speaking, these new observations would have to go into her exposé. Whatever mixture of drugs they were using on the patients here, that which was intended to sedate the unruly must include hallucinogens that actually drove the inmates further from sanity. Perhaps this was on purpose? To keep patients here as long as possible in order to draw in more financial support?

"An orderly will be back shortly with the keys to unlock the restraints. Once you are up again, please return to the common room," Nurse Ball stated as she exited the room and shut the door.

Nellie closed her eyes and let her head fall painfully to the side. With her limbs suspended for so many hours, her muscles ached horribly. Nellie shrieked. She had opened her eyes and now was looking squarely into Alice's red eyes, glowing sickly yellow at the edges. The horror's grimy hands gripped the edge of the gurney next to Nellie and she leaned in toward Nellie's face, her dripping, red maw opening.

Nellie couldn't breathe. Her entire body trembled violently and, with one last shudder, she lost consciousness.

CHAPTER 15

You remember my colleague, Fred Griffith?"

Nurse Murphy observed Dr. Braun on another walk with Nurse Ball. This meant there was important business at hand and they were not to be disturbed. They stepped through the front door on their way out to the path around the courtyard. "He's working on a fascinating new discovery: Genetic Material Encoding Virulence of Diplococcus."

"Genetic? What do you mean?" Nurse Ball's gait suddenly increased, forcing Dr. Braun to quicken his steps in order to keep pace.

"It's an amazing new science. It has been discovered

that our bodies actually carry genes with chromosomes, which appear to consist of polymers of both nucleic acids and proteins."

"And what's that got to do with Nellie?"

Detecting the edge in her voice, Dr. Braun caught her arm and stopped to face her. He continued in hushed tones. "I sent a sample of her blood to my dear friend to look into. It turns out that she has a unique pregnancy. Normally there are twenty-three paired chromosomes made up of forty-six total chromosomes donated from two sources, a mother and a father. Her baby has twenty-three paired chromosomes, but they are all identical to her mother's."

Nurse Ball sighed. "Please, let's pretend I have no medical training. What are you trying to say?"

"Nurse, the baby has no father."

"But that is not possible!" she scoffed.

A blood-curdling scream from somewhere inside the asylum rent the air.

"Speak of the devil! She is turning into a real handful," Nurse Ball muttered and, hiking her skirts up to her shins, rushed toward the asylum doors with Dr. Braun fast on her heels.

"She's perfect!" the doctor retorted, nearly leaping to keep up with Nurse Ball.

She shook her head as they made their way as quickly as possible through the door and along the long, dark corridors of the asylum to the seclusion room.

Nurse Ball stopped in front of the seclusion room door and turned back to face the doctor. With one hand on the doorknob, she looked at him and spoke in a pointed tone that she had never before dared to use with him. "I hope you know what you're doing."

Dr. Braun opened his mouth to speak, but such was his surprise that no words came out. She simply glowered at him, shook her head, and threw open the door.

Inside the seclusion room, several orderlies had already begun checking vital signs and restraints. "Marcus, what seems to be the matter with the patient?" Dr. Braun stepped into the room and slid his hands into his lab coat pockets.

"Nothing, sir. We couldn't find any reason for the episode. Everything in the room is as we left it ... it could not have been more than 10 minutes ago."

"Well then, perhaps the seclusion room's suspension was too much for her. Give her a sedative and we'll check her mental state again after she's rested up."

Nurse Ball waved toward a tray on the counter, which held a series of neatly arranged medical devices, including a full syringe. "Nothing out of the ordinary," she muttered.

Dr. Braun checked the young woman's pulse while the orderly carried out the directive to sedate her. Under Dr. Braun's fingertips, Nellie's pulse slowed. He pressed on her abdomen with his fingertips and palm, feeling each muscle and organ carefully.

"No abnormalities. Vital stats are good. Nurse Alissabeth," he spun toward the staff member hovering quietly near the medical tray. "Did you see anything?"

She swallowed and swiped her bangs away from her forehead. "Well, there was one curious note. She was babbling something about someone named Alice."

Nurse Ball shot the doctor a hard look. "How could she know about Alice? Did you say something she could have overheard?"

Dr. Braun motioned the staff to leave, and they were all too eager to comply. Nurse Alissabeth shut the door behind her without a backward glance, leaving the prostrate and unconscious Nellie alone with Nurse Ball and the doctor.

Nurse Ball glared at the doctor as he removed his spectacles to polish them on the edge of his sleeve.

"Nellie just doesn't fit the profile of the other Alice sightings. She has no history of head trauma. While she might be a little underweight, she's hardly on death's door. But she is adding a new element to the puzzle: her freak pregnancy."

"I still don't see how it's possible to be pregnant without a father." Nurse Ball folded her arms across her chest and looked down her nose.

"It's called parthenogenesis: the 'virgin birth.' A relatively new field of study, although, if the Bible is to be believed, the phenomenon has been around for at least two thousand."

He watched Nellie breath shallowly for a few moments, studying her pale face. "I have a hunch that this child of Nellie's may be gifted. Maybe it has the same freak genetic mutation as Dorothy and Alice."

Again Nurse Ball's heart skipped a beat at the mention of the little girl's name. She remained silent as she reflected on which words she would choose next. "What makes you think Dorothy is like Alice?"

"I have seen it with my own eyes. I suspect the answers to Project Alice will lie in the meta link between Dorothy and Nellie. We should get them into the tank immediately." Dr. Braun replaced his spectacles and smiled. The smile was not warm and welcoming to Nurse Ball. Instead, it was cold, mechanical. What, perhaps, an automaton might use to display a gesture of encouragement.

Nurse Ball inserted the black iron key into the keyhole and twisted it, sending the tumblers inside into an organized row. She twisted the brass knob on the door labeled "HYPNOTIC INDUCTION ROOM 1" and pushed the door open with a solid thrust of her shoulder. With a resistant groan, the heavy door on rusted hinges opened most of the way before coming to a grinding halt in the groove of the cement floor.

Nurse Ball turned back to the gurney and pulled Nellie through the doorway into the mildewed room full of machinery, water tanks, gears, wires and hoses. Nurse Alissabeth pushed the other end of the gurney in and shut the door. Her key scraped in the lock, the noise reverberating throughout the large, dank, cement chamber.

Dr. Braun poured a perfect white stream of Epsom salts into the liquid solution swishing about inside the brass tank walls. The liquid's surface appeared to be partially solid, like curdled milk, with dissolving salt chunks.

The nurses carefully connected the straps on Nellie's prone body to a set of dangling chains, which were attached to a pulley system. Having first been suspended in the Seclusion Room, she was now to be hoisted from the gurney and into the water in the tank. With Nellie's body hovering inches above the water, Dr. Braun slipped a mask over her eyes, nose and mouth.

Nurse Alissabeth cranked the metal ring at the top of the oxygen tank one full turn, and cool oxygen hissed through the tubing and into Nellie's face mask. Nurse Ball poured a bucket of warm liquid into the tank and nodded to the doctor. "Ready." She spoke gruffly to the doctor. He noted wryly, she would not make eye contact with him. He nodded to Nurse Alissabeth, and together they lowered Nellie into the tank.

Warm water washed over Nellie, the sloshing water surrounding her instantly bringing her to a panicked consciousness. She flailed her arms and legs, crying out, into the mask.

"Nellie, calm down this instant! This is your treatment now!" Dr. Braun spoke slowly and loudly, yet Nellie could not hear a word.

As far as Nellie could discern, she was completely immersed in water, and naked save for the hoses and tubes connected to her limbs. She struggled desperately, air bubbles churning around her body.

Dr. Braun sighed. "Make sure Dorothy is in position."

Nellie stopped thrashing long enough to peer through the milky white goggles of her mask. She could just barely make out Dr. Braun's distorted form standing next to the tank, his hands on his hips.

Nurse Alissabeth stepped to the flotation tank adjacent to Nellie's and peered through the windows.

"Patient Gale is ready," she announced.

"Good. Let's get started."

Nellie watched the doctor lower his arms and step away. But there, in the void that he left, stood a familiar silhouette about the size of a little girl.

Dr. Braun and the nurses stepped out of the large chamber and into a separate room behind a glass window. The room contained all manner of switches, knobs and buttons that only the doctor knew how to manipulate. Nellie had been left alone again, trapped. Inside her mask, her heavy breathing was the only sound as she stared at the silhouette of the little girl. It stepped closer. Nellie pulled frantically at the hoses holding her in place in her watery tomb, the sound of her breathing becoming deafening inside the mask.

Suddenly, Alice's hands pressed up against the window next to Nellie, and the shrill, raspy voice shrieked in her ears.

"She can't take you away from me! You're mine! ... Mine ...."

"HELP!" Nellie cried out, into the mask. "Please help! It's Alice! She's coming for me!"

Dr. Braun pressed and held down a green button. His voice was distorted and uneven as it echoed into the tank through a tinny speaker.

"Just relax, Nellie. It's not going to hurt. Your subconscious mind is playing tricks on you." Nurse

Ball handed Dr. Braun a writing pad and pen. He jotted the date and time.

"Get ready — we're about to begin. How's Ms. Gale?"

"Stable, doctor. I'm getting some currents on the lateralization. Right hemisphere dominant ... I think she's asleep."

"Good. Let's set up the meta link."

"But Ms. Bly is still fluctuating," Nurse Ball interjected.

Dr. Braun pushed and held the green button again. "Miss Bly ... can you hear me? I need you to relax." Dr. Braun released the button, waiting for a response.

But no response came.

"Miss Bly?"

His query was met with a death-defying screech from somewhere near Nellie's tank. Dr. Braun jumped, and Nurse Ball took a step back, her hand lightly resting over her heart.

"What the hell was that?" she rushed toward the tank window.

Nellie had begun to speak to someone. She was no longer panicked, but now seemed to be peacefully floating in her liquid solution.

"Dorothy ... I can see you ..." she whispered.

Dr. Braun raised his hand to stop Nurse Ball from leaving. They both leaned in, listening intently.

"Dorothy, you're in a place ... it looks like ..." Nellie murmured.

Dr. Braun held up his hand and whispered to the nurses, "She's in. It's working." He began to furiously scribble the words that were spoken between Nellie and Dorothy.

"Finally ..." he breathed, "progress!"

CHAPTER 16

N ellie found herself standing alone on a brick road in an utterly foreign countryside. She seemed to be somewhere outdoors, beneath a gray sky filled with dark clouds that threatened an oncoming storm, each intermittently illuminated from within by flashes of blue light.

The brick path beneath her feet twisted and turned to oddly meander through unkempt, wild grass as tall as corn stalks. The grimy, faded, yellowish-brown bricks weren't even placed in rows, but rather had been dropped into the ground at odd angles. Patches of bricks were simply gone, having been broken and worn away with time. Nellie squinted and knelt down to touch the bricks. Was this another dream?

Each remaining brick contained the imprint of a human face that was contorted in agony. She touched the ridge of one face's cheek, traced over the grimacing eyes of another. Here was a face frozen mid-scream. Next there was a half-broken brick, its eyes rolled up and back in horror to see the crack running through its forehead.

Hearing a rustling noise just ahead, she realized that she was not alone. Nellie shot to her feet and peered through the darkness past gnarled, overgrown tree branches just in time to see a familiar figure dart over a hill.

"Dorothy!" Nellie called, but she was not heard. She couldn't see Dorothy anymore. The anguish in the girl's voice floated over the eerie, broken, brick road and the wild growth.

"Oh, my! No, No! What has happened to my dear Oz?"

"Dorothy, wait!" Nellie called and dashed up the road after Dorothy as fast as she could manage. "Wait, it's me! It's Nell!"

She came to the top of the hill and skidded to a stop. Before her, the landscape opened up into a terrifying array of labyrinthine passages that stretched as far as the eye could see. They were illuminated in red and shadowed in black, the walls lined with murky display cases.

Dorothy's tiny figure, far ahead in the distance, disappeared into an opening in the massive labyrinth. Nellie charged down the path after her, struggling to keep that opening in sight.

Dr. Braun pulled a long and trailing piece of paper through a feed in his machine and peered over the top of his spectacles at the results being transmitted in beeps and scratches.

"Excellent! We have established a Meta Link between Nellie and Dorothy. Nellie is experiencing Dorothy's world now, as we speak!"

"All vitals are stable," Nurse Alissabeth confirmed, reading over the row of lights on her side of the control room.

"This is amazing!" Braun grinned and turned around to share his excitement with Nurse Ball. She flipped a piece of paper over on the medical chart in her hands and gave no response.

Dr. Braun cleared his throat and turned his attention back to his writing pad and pen.

Nurse Ball flipped her clipboard over for another look. Yes, this was her clipboard. Yet, somehow, the page in front of her was not a form for tracking the vital signs of a patient during therapeutic procedures. This was a bizarre sketch of a girl marching steadfast toward something unseen, surrounded by an army of what appeared to be ... demons?

Nurse Ball ripped the drawing from the clipboard, crumpled it up, and tossed it into the wastebin.

STORM OF ALICE

Nellie dashed through the opening of the labyrinth and quickly checked the halls left, right and center. No sign of Dorothy ... except for a blue ribbon that was lying on the path to her right. She took a deep breath and searched for any sign of movement down the branching passageways, which stretched on and on into darkness.

She had to be careful to find a way to differentiate one hall from the next, and to trace where she had already been. Nellie picked up a broken yellow brick from the entrance to the labyrinth and found the first of the display cases that lined the wall on her right. Inside its smudged, glass doors were antiquated china dolls in checkered blue dresses and perfect brown braids. They sat askew, leaning on one another, each with a crack running through its fragile, chipped head. Some dolls were completely missing the tops of their heads, with only their red, shiny lips and a bone-white chins remaining above their necks.

Nellie took the heavy brick and smashed it against the glass case. The glass cracked in a spider-web pattern.

Satisfied, Nellie picked up the blue ribbon, dropped it in her pocket, and charged down the hallway until she felt the need to catch her breath. Panting heavily, she stopped in front of another display case that was filled with china pigs that had been burnt and blackened. She drew back the brick.

WHIRRRR, WHIRRRR, WHIRRRR, CLANK!

Nellie spun about and came face to face with the manufacturer of the mechanical clattering.

"Did ... you ... do ... this ... to ... us?" the dreadful vision before her struggled to speak, its voice imprisoned by the timing of its mechanized whirring gears and ticking sprockets.

Nellie clapped her hand to her mouth to keep from crying out. The thing's human skin intertwined with its rusted tin panels and lengths of chain, and angry, red flesh bubbled over the edges of its twisted, black pipes and metallic skeletal armatures. Large, pointed hooks jutted out from under its rib cage and seeped a pungent, yellow secretion. The inner workings of its abdomen were completely exposed by a large, plastic bubble, inside which a robotic fetus squirmed.

Nellie stepped back and turned to run, but the automaton grabbed her with a metal hand and pitched her into the display case with such force that the glass shattered on contact. Nellie slid to the ground like a rag doll, crying out as pain exploded from her back and surged throughout her body. Before she could move out of the way, the metal monster picked her up and hoisted her over its head.

"This —" it spun her roughly around, high in the air" — this ... is ... your ... fault!"

CLANK, CLANK, CLANK!

"What is my fault?" she cried.

It gave no answer. With each heavy, mechanical footfall, it carried Nellie deeper into the red labyrinth. Tears streamed down her hot cheeks, as, once again, she found herself utterly helpless against the horrors of Bedlam. Not knowing where she was or how she had arrived, she had no earthly idea how she could possibly escape.

The monstrosity turned a corner, and the hall opened up into a chamber that contained several entryways. The further in they went, the more the labyrinth looked like a mausoleum. The thing clanked forward, into the center of the chamber, retaining the limp Nellie in its elevated grasp.

In each doorway, a fresh horror appeared to join the tin man who held her prisoner. In one doorway stood a thing that looked vaguely like a scarecrow. It towered fifteen feet tall and wore a floppy, black hat that shaded a dead face whose skin was decayed and stretched over long and broken teeth. Its arms swung at absurd lengths, the hands grasping human body parts which it was stuffing in the gaping hole of its abdomen, straight into its bulging intestines.

The next doorway revealed a mangled lion. Hooks and chains embedded in its flesh pilled its skin apart in places. The lion walked, with some difficulty, on two legs, one of which was latched tightly inside the big black iron teeth of a bear trap.

It used its giant claws to pull in vain at other wicked hunters' traps that latched to its torso and dripped rivulets of bright, red blood. Around its neck was a thick, black, spiked, leather collar whose edges cut into its neck, leaving raw, infected welts. It pulled at the collar and tossed its head angrily, eyes flashing green. It glared at Nellie and growled, causing the long scar that crossed its face to wrinkle as it spoke.

"You. You've tainted us," the lion's deep rumbling voice resounded throughout the chamber. It swung its head and lifted its lip to reveal huge, deadly teeth. "You've tainted Oz."

In the next doorway appeared a witch who was brandishing a riding crop in one hand and a whip in the other. Her hands were adorned by long, sharp claws that were painted a shiny, blood red. She stood upon impossibly high-heeled boots, so wickedly pointed at the toes that they surely could be used to eviscerate any enemy. Her black, buttoned dress had been torn to shreds and hung limply about her green frame like black tissue paper.

She hissed at Nellie and snapped the whip in the dirt next to her, causing a cloud of dust to rise at her feet.

"You NEVER should have come here, girlie."

An obscenely wide, evil, red grin spread across her green face and caused her already pointed nose to extend even further downward. With unnaturally long strides, she quickly closed the distance between them, flicking her whip back and forth with every step. An unearthly screech filled the air, causing every creature to hunker down. The lion clapped its giant paws over its ragged ears, and the witch froze in her tracks.

Nellie was dumped unceremoniously to the ground. She lifted her head, trying to find the source of the awful sound.

There, shrouded in the darkness of the far corner of the chamber, stood the small, yet terrifying figure that she knew would soon glide forth from the blackest of shadows. Nellie's stomach turned and writhed with nausea. The off-key singing began once more:

"You are scared, Nellie Bly," young Alice said,
"And your hair is turning quite white;

The Scarecrow bent and lifted his head in the small figure's direction in a fluid snakelike motion. Its papery voice rattled like dry dead leaves lifted by a hot breeze. "Another one?"

The eerie song floated through the chamber around them from the dark shadows:

Yet you worry and fret you're not right in the head—
Do you think you might perish from fright?"

The mechanical man clunked backward one heavy step at a time, gears whirring and head cocking to the left and to the right. "Unclean."

"In this place," Nellie Bly replied to the girl,
"I feared I might have a bad brain;

He halted and shook violently, then collapsed to the floor — nuts, screws and pieces of tin clattering to the ground around him. He pulled himself along, dragging his body, and continued his shaky, measured retreat, all the time repeating, "Unclean, unclean, unclean … ."

"We must warn Dorothy," the witch hissed, taking another unnaturally long step backward to the doorway and out of the chamber.

The earth beneath Nellie's hands and feet began to rumble and shake. Saliva dripping from the corner of her slack mouth, Nellie lifted her chin from the dust to find Alice gliding toward her from the corner.

The earth shook, the walls crumbled, plaster fell in chunks, and bricks toppled to the floor. The labyrinth and everything within this land was falling to pieces.

But, now that I'm perfectly sure I have none,
Why worry that I've gone quite insane."

Alice was close enough now that Nellie could see her dark-red lips part and spread into a smile. That was all it took.

Nellie screamed at the top of her lungs with all of the power she could muster.

"ALLLIIICCCCCEEEE! STAY BACK!"

The liquid surrounding Nellie churned and bubbled with her wild thrashing. Her mask slipped off in the tumult and left her choking on the briny fluid in place of the air she so badly needed. She inhaled and gagged, hiccupping and clawing at the tank walls in her desperation to snatch just one breath of air.

"Get her out of there! Get her out before she drowns!" Nurse Ball shrieked, running toward the tank.

Dr. Braun and Nurse Alissabeth followed fast on her heels and tugged frantically at the rattling chains, trying to lift Nellie out of the fluid. Her thrashing, and the sheer effort of pulling a body from a viscous liquid, left the three struggling with every ounce of strength to free Nellie. Bubbles frothed and churned around her metal prison, as Nellie became hopelessly tangled in the mass of rubber tubing.

With one heave that lifted her briefly from the floor, Nurse Ball threw her full weight onto the chain, enabling the three to finally hoist Nellie from the vacuum of the liquid in the tank. They dropped her, like a wet fish, onto the nearby gurney, where she flailed and gasped for air.

Nurse Ball put her hands on Nellie's shoulders and spoke in a soothing tone.

"It's alright now Nellie, you're back. Shhhhhhh ... ." She held Nellie down gently until the thrashing slowed.

Nurse Alissabeth administered a sedative into Nellie's arm, and the familiar wave of warmth carried Nellie off into unconsciousness.

Still trying to catch his breath, Dr. Braun nodded and waved a hand at the gurney. Nurse Alissabeth returned the gesture, nodded her understanding, and, with a sturdy shove, wheeled Nellie to the door.

Nurse Ball spun around with her hands on her hips, eyes flashing. "What the hell was that?!"

Dr. Braun pulled a handkerchief from his pocket and dabbed at his forehead. He waited for the other nurse to unlock the door and wheel the gurney out before he spoke.

"The Meta Link was established. Nellie made it into Dorothy's world and saw it all firsthand."

"I see!" Nurse Ball nodded, thrusting her hand into the air. "And do you have some creative explanation for why Alice was there too?"

Dr. Braun glanced up at Nurse Ball and then back down into his handkerchief as if the answer might be hidden therein.

"Perhaps Nellie's child shares the same 'gifts' as Dorothy and Alice. Perhaps that is how Alice is able to communicate with her?"

"Well *perhaps* you should get your facts in order before pushing on ahead with any more half-cocked theories! These patients are people, doctor, not dolls to play with. I was under the impression that the point was to try to cure them of their ills!"

Nurse Ball snatched the handkerchief from the doctor's fumbling hands and threw it in his face before storming from the room.

He frowned at the handkerchief again. He did not like the way Nurse Ball had emphasized the word "doctor" in such a mocking tone.

CHAPTER 17

D r. Braun stepped into his office, shut his door, and locked it behind him. He crossed to the open window, slammed it shut, slapped the shutters closed, and fell into his rolling office chair to bury his head in his hands. He was so close to bringing all of the pieces together. He had, slowly but surely, learned what would work and what would not. But now past mistakes returned to haunt him with a vengeance. Things were in such a precarious state, and if something went wrong with Nellie or Dorothy right now —

RING! RING!

Dr. Braun jumped, causing a multitude of papers to fly from his desk to flutter to the floor. He fumbled with the receiver on his candlestick telephone and brought it to his ear.

"Yes! Hello!" he leaned in toward the mouthpiece while adjusting his spectacles.

"Yes, Dr. Braun. This is the operator. You have a call from a Dr. Fred Griffith. Shall I put it through?"

"Ah, yes, put him through," he sat up straight and tugged his jacket smartly into place, smoothing the lapel.

After a series of clicks, Dr. Griffith's voice came over the line.

"Good evening, Dr. Braun."

"Good evening, Dr. Griffith. What news do you have for me?"

"Henry, I have been working on the blood samples you have given me. The results are just not possible!"

"Go on, Fred."

"The chromosomes are completely mixed up. There is a freak anomaly in the XY pairs. You were right, these patients … they have no fathers. In my lifetime, I never thought to see one virgin birth, much less four. I must meet them!"

Dr. Braun rose and stepped away from the desk, carrying the telephone as far as the cord would allow. Rocking back and forth on the balls of his feet, he finally said, "I'm sorry, Fred. My patients are in a very delicate part of their treatment."

There was a moment of silence before Dr. Griffith spoke, "You're not experimenting on Project: Alice again are you?"

Dr. Braun scowled. "That's confidential."

"Henry, you can't possibly think of continuing those …" he paused, searching for the best light to put on the forthcoming negative phrase, "… highly unethical experiments."

Dr. Braun set the telephone back down and fell into his chair. He pulled off his spectacles and rubbed his eyes. "Don't worry. This time, I have everything under control."

Nellie awoke in her cot, her head positively swimming. She sniffed at her wrist and confirmed that her skin smelled salty, like the liquid in the tank. Her memory was intact. Her stomach twisted and growled. When was the last time she had eaten? And where was Dorothy now?

Wind rattled the glass of the narrow slit window. She pulled herself to her feet and stood, tip-toe, on the edge of her cot to see outside. Dark clouds obscured the stars and the moon, but she could see the tree tops whipping to and fro in the wind — storm coming.

Nellie stepped down from the cot, pulled it aside, and knelt down to feel for the loose brick. She needed to get to her report and record everything she had seen. Whether the vision had been drug-induced or not she would leave to consider at a later date.

She groggily pulled the folded papers from the hole in the wall and spread them on the floor in front of her, along with her trusty crayons. Putting a red crayon to the page, she tried to press down to write, but the crayon slipped from her loose fingers and rolled across the floor.

Nellie reached through the fogginess that enveloped her mind, which was no doubt due to the recently administered drugs. Wait ...

She picked up the pages and held them close to her eyes, trying to see in the scant light. These were not her notes. These were pictures. She opened her eyes wide and flipped through the folded pages.

Where once her words had been, there now were illustrations. And not just any drawings ... these were from the same hand that had wrought the pictures in Alice's corridor ... in her dreams.

Roughly sketched, in pencil, was an angelic Dorothy standing before a lion, a scarecrow, and a tin man.

The next sketch depicted the horrific tin creature that had held her captive just hours before.

DOROTHY GALE OF OZ

THE TIN MAN

Had she drawn these in a drugged state? Her morbid curiosity led her to turn the page and examine the next disturbing drawing: a cat demon chimera emerging from ... a doorway?

She reached for the next set of folded papers, and paused. There, on the floor before her was a trail of fresh, red blood.

Nellie held her breath and followed the trail ... it led to her stomach. She cried out, looking at her dress and all around her body. The blood was smeared down the bed, across the floor, and out under the door.

Nellie's door was being unlocked. The door itself began to open with a creak, casting a shaft of eerie green light across the floor and over the trail of blood.

The silhouette of a young girl stood framed in the doorway, instantly sending an icy-cold finger of fear down Nellie's neck and back. She froze.

But it was a different little girl's voice that spoke.

"The bad men are coming."

"Rose? Is that you?" Nellie crawled toward the open door.

Meeeeeooooooowwwwrrrr ...

Rose breathed in sharply and turned toward the mewling sound.

"Oh!" She turned away from the door, and then the sound of her small, bare feet pitter-patted down the hall. "I can't let them catch me!" she puffed, her voice echoing back down the hall to Nellie.

"Rose! Wait!" Nellie cried out, scrambling to get to her feet and follow the small girl. She stumbled into the hall and held on to the wall. Patients in the adjacent rooms were all asleep; no doubt enjoying their narcotic slumber. She briefly wondered if they weren't all part of a nightmarish landscape wherein a lion, a tin man, a scarecrow, a witch, and a terrifying little girl could haunt them no matter where they tried to hide. Or, perhaps, the drugs had made them so numb that they couldn't dream at all.

Meeeooowwwwwwwww ...

A cat's mewling pulled Nellie from her hazy inner dialog and drew her attention back to the hallway in front of her. She hadn't seen any cats on the island before, but she supposed it was possible that a staff member had brought a pet to Bedlam and it had somehow gotten loose.

Rose giggled from somewhere nearby, perhaps the main common room. Nellie turned the corner, treading softly. She slipped along the wall and glanced toward the asylum entrance just in time to see the little girl with the brown curls dart in front of the main door.

Meeeeeooooooowwwwrrrr ...

The cat's voice drifted to Nellie from down a hall. She imagined a small tabby cat brushing against a table leg in the common room, quizzically calling for someone to kindly place a saucer of cold milk on the floor, please. Nellie tiptoed toward the asylum entrance in the main lobby and passed in front of the great, gold looking-glass.

CRAAAACCCKKKK!

She splayed flat against the wall. The high-pitched cracking of glass sounded as though a window had just shattered. She glanced all around, but the windows were all as they were before. But it hadn't been a window after all. It was the looking-glass.

There, dead center in the once perfect, framed piece was a ghastly crack. Nellie searched the room for the cause. As if in answer to her question, lines began to draw themselves into the mirror. One after the other, letters appeared, as if invisible, clawed fingers were scratching them into the glass from the other side.

EreH ERa eW

The letters were difficult to read,; they were backwards. She reached into her pocket and pulled out the caterpillar locket. She opened the tiny catch with her fingernail and popped it carefully open. Turning to look into the mirrored surface of the locket, she saw the words reflected:

We aRE HerE

Pressed to the glass behind the words, a demonic, twisted face stared back at her, pushing and contorting, smearing grisly filth on the glass in its efforts to squeeze through the crack in the mirror. Nellie gasped and snapped the locket shut. Spinning around to the mirror, she was prepared to face whatever awaited. Yet now there was nothing in the mirror except her reflection. The words, demon — gone.

Nellie leaned against the wall, pressing her temples with both palms and squeezing her eyes shut. Was this the drugs? The line between reality and fantasy had become so thoroughly blurred that she did not know whether or not to trust her own eyes.

Meowwwwwww ...

Nellie looked toward the sound and caught a glimpse of Rose's dress as it disappeared around the corner. "Rose!" she called out softly, and hurried after her. The door to the basement steam tunnels stood ajar. Nellie slid to a stop before she reached the door. It creaked open a bit wider.

"Rose?" she called out again from the doorway and then peered down the stairs. The little girl's faint giggle answered from somewhere in the darkness below. She put her foot down on the first creaky stair, and uttered an inaudible curse. Down each step she crept, descending deeper into the bowels of Bedlam.

BANG!

Nellie spun around to look to the top of the staircase where the door had just slammed shut, but found no one there. Most likely an orderly on the night-shift had passed by and noticed the open door. But that soft sound of laughter — was that the orderly — or something else?

On the bottom stair, she reached out her toe and felt for the floor beneath. Yes, there it was, cold and dirty. She pressed her bare foot flat onto the basement corridor floor. There was faint light down here, cast by the occasional flickering light bulb. Creosote dripped from the walls, creating unsettling patterns that resembled faces and creatures.

Was that a burst of laughter? Or just the wind? Nellie's breathing quickened as she trod through the dim corridor.

MEOWWWW!

Had the cat followed her down the stairs? Or were there more cats in the basement? Nellie spun in circles, frantically glancing about in the darkness. She backed into the pipes that lined the corridor wall, and they moaned in protest.

Wait ... the rust dripping from the pipes ... this was all very familiar ... .

And there it was, at the end of the corridor, just as it had always been in her dreams. The vault. And, in front of it, the unmistakable figure of Alice. The light bulb above the vault door flickered, providing just enough light to make out the grisly details of the face that was partially obscured by the stringy gnarls of hair.

Her red eyes peered up at Nellie.

"You found me, Nellie. Just like I knew you would."

Nellie stared in horror, unable to move. This wasn't a dream. This wasn't a hallucination. Her feet were glued to the floor, yet her limbs were electric with fear.

"Where — where's Rose?" she whispered.

"They were going to kill her," the raspy voice replied. Nellie realized that Alice's lips did not move. She could somehow hear Alice's voice inside her head.

"You should thank me," the voice continued, "I'm keeping her safe for you."

A menacing growl emerged from the darkness, somewhere behind Nellie. She glanced fleetingly over her shoulder, unwilling to turn her back on Alice. Something human-like moved in the shadows. "Who are you? Show yourself!" she called out forcefully, over the tremor in her voice.

In the darkness, Nellie could just make out the outline of something that stood on two legs. The thing hunched over and twisted back and forth, writhing and stretching.

"He will in just a moment," the voice in Nellie's head replied. Nellie looked at Alice again and saw the corners of the fetid, red lips curl upward into a sort of smile.

Nellie looked back to the form, which had begun to shake violently. It staggered toward her and into the dim pool of light, revealing remnants of a human form, its skin blistering and peeling away as something under the skin pushed its way out.

"Come join us." Alice held up a hand and beckoned Nellie toward her. Her lips still did not move; her chin hung close to her chest. She looked up at Nellie through blood-red eyes and grinned. Nellie could see her pointed, crimson tongue running over the jagged edges of her broken teeth. "We can all play together."

A fur-like body broke through the creature's human skin with a sickening pop. Wet, pulpy layers of adipose and skin fell away.

ROWWWWRRRRR!

Claws pushed through the fingertips of the human hand, splitting the skin and exposing mangy, gray-and-black, striped fur. The long, sharp teeth jutting from the feline countenance chewed and gnawed the human finger exteriors away from the paw and spit them into a bloody pile on the dirt floor.

"Dear God..." Nellie whispered.

The giant cat emerged almost completely from its rotting flesh cocoon in the shadows.

"No, silly. Not God. It's my friend, the Cheshire cat!" Alice grinned and rolled her red eyes. "He wants to play with you."

A high-pitched scream rang out from the corridor behind them. "Rose?" Nellie cried out, unable to mask her terror.

"She's with me, Nellie" Alice's scratchy voice spat. Nellie looked back at Alice who now glowered at her and pointed down the corridor. "Open the doors." Her hands dropped lifelessly down to her sides and she grinned with wide, scarlet eyes, her head cocking suddenly to the side. "Come on Nellie. We're waiting." Alice drifted backward, melting through the vault door into nothingness.

"Alice?" Nellie said, her whole body trembling. "Alice?"

An unnatural, shrill howling caused Nellie to turn and face the creature in the shadows again. The howl sustained its high note for a few moments before shuddering and dropping into a deep, guttural growl. She could, see by the beast's silhouette, that the hackles on the back of its neck were rising. The sounds it was emitting were those of a cat that is tensed to attack.

"Nice kitty." Nellie moved cautiously toward her only escape route: the space between the wall and the enormous feline.

RrrrreeeeeeeEEEEEOOOWWRRRR!

The cat leapt out from the gloom, its enormous fangs bared and its murderous claws extended toward Nellie's throat. Nellie's movements were pure survival instinct. She ducked and crouched against the wall just in time for the giant, cat-like demon to fly past her and slam into the vault door. It shook its massive head back and forth and scrambled to stand upright.

In the light, Nellie could see that this was a human-shaped beast with a feline head. When it turned back toward her, she stared directly into eyes as black as death and its lunatic ear-to-ear grin full of colossal, razor-sharp, metallic teeth. Blood and pus dripped from open wounds on its side; its diseased skin was covered in burns and infected boils. Its face a mask of death, its body a moving disease, its maniacal grin — this was surely the essence of madness.

The Cheshire cat swung its head and shoulders toward her as it readied for another pounce. Its black eyes rolled and it resumed its deep-throated growl, as it tensed to spring. Saliva spewed from the corners of its monstrous mouth.

Nellie sprang from the floor and sprinted as fast as her shaking legs could carry her down the corridor.

The cat demon threw its head back and yowled, the force of its powerful voice rending Nellie's ears. It dropped to all fours and sprang forward, leaping down the corridor after her.

Nellie had never run as fast as she did now. In mere seconds, she arrived at the bottom of the stairs and leapt up the steps two-by-two toward the light that shone under the door at the top of the stairs. The cat yowled again and leapt toward Nellie, claws extended. The tips of its claws sliced cleanly through the skin of her calf as she bounded to the next stair. She felt a sharp pain, but such was her terror that it didn't slow her gait one bit. She kicked open the basement door, destroying the lock, and slammed into the opposite wall, panting.

"HEEELLLPPPPPP!" she shrieked, as she sprinted at break-neck speed toward the front desk. She just had to find people — it didn't matter who. But something tackled Nellie from the side and knocked her down, falling upon her and cracking her head against the black

-and -white tiled floor. For Nellie, everything instantly went black.

Nurse Ball, clad in a nightgown and robe, hovered over Nellie, who was lying, sprawled and unconscious, on the Seclusion Room gurney. Nurse Chiu applied pressure to the small cut over Nellie's eyebrow. This injury, from Dr. Carandini's vase, had almost healed over, but now blood trickled from the reopened wound.

Dr. Braun stood opposite Nurse Ball, folding his arms over his chest. He still wore his business clothing and lab coat, which were a bit wrinkled and disheveled at this late hour. Lost in thought, he stared down at Nellie and stroked his beard.

"She was saying that Alice was after her when we caught her." Nurse Ball smoothed back a few rampant hairs that protruded from her sleeping cap.

Dr. Braun glanced up at her. "Where did you say you found her?"

"She had somehow gotten down into the basement."

He paused, looking hard at Nellie again.

"Wake Dorothy up. We're proceeding to the Electrolysis Room."

Nurse Ball's jaw dropped open. "At this hour?"

Dr. Braun turned to her, arms still folded across his chest. "Nurse Ball, if you have any problems with the treatments I am prescribing for my patients or the time at which I choose to administer them, you know exactly when and where to catch the next ferry. If you choose to continue to practice medicine with me, then meet me in the Electrolysis Room immediately." He turned on his heel, pushed Nellie's gurney toward the door, and wheeled her out into the hallway.

Nurse Chiu quietly collected the tray of medical tools and glanced up at Nurse Ball, whose mouth remained agape. Nurse Chiu carried the tray to the door, and, with a private smile, exited the room.

Nellie's eyes fluttered. She came to and became aware that she was on a gurney, being wheeled somewhere. Cautiously, she opened her eyes and saw the hallway and a series of doorways. This was a hallway she did not recognize. The doors were all open. Peering into the room to her left, she saw a naked inmate strapped to a table. The female patient's body was covered with small, precise incisions, each of which dripped blood into grooves on the tabletop. Next to this table, an inmate wore a leather collar that was attached to the end of a pole held by an orderly. The inmate was being forced to walk endlessly on a platform with a rolling surface. These devices were attached to a large, tangled pile of wire. Two small, blue eyes peeped out at Nellie from the mess of wires, as her gurney rolled past this doorway.

"Help me!" Rose's voice called from somewhere in the room. Nellie struggled to sit up but Dr. Braun gently pushed her back down. The door to Rose's room began to swing shut, and the pale face and red eyes that stared back at her from the doorway told her who was closing the door. Her gurney eventually reached a door labeled "Hypnotic Induction Room 2." Here was another of Dr. Braun's bizarre rooms, filled with elaborate mechanisms.

Dr. Braun positioned Nellie's gurney next to another, on which lay Dorothy, arms by her sides. She turned and saw Nellie, her wide, wet eyes spilling tears.

"Be brave, Dorothy," Nellie nodded to her.

Dorothy nodded, but her head trembled and her hands shook.

Nurse Ball entered the room, still wrapped in her flannel robe. She slid a rubber bite guard into Nellie's mouth and taped it tightly to her teeth. As the nurse secured Nellie's arms with leather straps, Dr. Braun crossed to a control panel and flipped a switch. The machine, labeled "Dynamo," sprang to life with a whirring, clanking sound.

He looked over his shoulder and spoke to Nurse Ball.

"Check all neuro connectors. We're ready to go."

The orderlies performed a final check of the table-leg wire as Dr. Braun adjusted and checked Nellie's metal head restraint. Satisfied, he made his way to the Observation Room. Nurse Ball scurried after him, whispering. "Doctor, you know that this is exactly what sent Alice over the edge!"

"I've modified the procedure since then. Now, we are using electrical currents to create a Soul Link between the two women."

"A Soul Link?"

"The previous experiment established the Meta Link, which allowed Dorothy to bring Nellie into her fantasy world. The Soul Link takes that bond one step further. It not only allows Nellie to enter Dorothy's world, but also enables her to actually become part of it, essentially transforming Nellie into a tamer version of Dorothy."

"And this will help them both how?" Nurse Ball blinked.

Dr. Braun nodded to an orderly, who, in turn, pulled a switch. Nellie's eyes filled with a blinding flash of blue light, which sent waves of indescribable pain screaming from her head, down her spine, and out through every pore of her body. She convulsed and shrieked through the rubber bite guard, her cries echoed by Dorothy's.

CHAPTER 18

Nellie stood once more upon the broken and worn bricks of Dorothy's world. Oz, she had called it, when Nellie was last here with her. The sky, again, was ominously overcast, with intermittent flashes of blue light splintering the black clouds. The sound of rolling thunder echoed in the distance. She now found herself on a different section of the dingy yellow road. Ahead, the path lead up to a pair of enormous, dark-green gates embedded in crumbling, emerald -green walls. The broken gates hung wide open.

She followed the path into the decimated city. Burnt and twisted bodies littered the landscape. Buildings that had once surrounded a palace were reduced to rubble or simply swallowed whole by earth.

There was no sign of Dorothy anywhere.

Nellie stepped cautiously through the debris, side-stepping rubble which, like the bricks in the road, was etched with contorted faces of Oz's inhabitants writhing in agony and despair. It was apparent that this Emerald City had once been majestic and beauteous, yet it somehow had been reduced to blackened ruins. Only the palace remained, flanked by two large monuments and guarded by gargantuan, locked gates. Statues, stones, mannequins, and bodies all had been burnt by an apocalyptic fire. A thick coat of soot covered the ground, and dark rainwater dripped down shattered walls.

Nellie looked for any sign of life that could point her to Dorothy. Not too far away, a solitary small structure remained intact. Dilapidated though it looked, it was a house in which she might find someone who could provide an explanation and perhaps a clue to Dorothy's whereabouts.

Nellie ran to the lone house in the midst of the soot- and rubble-strewn city. It was a modest, built-to-be-cozy domicile with a welcoming porch and bright-green shutters on all of the windows. But, like everything else in Oz, it had decayed. An old-fashioned sign swung back and forth in the breeze, its rusty hinges squeaking in protest. The stenciled lettering read:

Nellie gently pushed open the green front door. It obligingly swung open on its last remaining hinge, and, with a groan, splintered away from the frame and clattered to the ground in a cloud of dust.

Contrary to the house's cheerful exterior, the interior was dark. The chandelier in the entryway was constructed with black crystals, and the curtains and fabrics were abysmal tones of black, crimson, and midnight green.

The walls were lined with faded photographs of smiling families. One in particular caught her attention. A young, beautiful girl with long hair, bright eyes, and a dimpled grin sat beneath a flowering tree, a happy tabby cat on her lap. The photograph had been taken from too great a distance for it to show the girl's face in detail, but her size and form looked vaguely familiar.

"Could it be?" Nellie breathed, touching the picture.

As she marveled at each of the many photographs, the breeze through the ramshackle house carried with it a horrible stench. Nellie plugged her nose and stepped into the living area. She was met with a sight that made her gag.

The carcasses of humans, scavenged from the road outside, were artistically arranged with barbed-wire, twine, and tape. Some of their body parts had been tightly ensconced in sheer cloth, but not enough to completely cover their grief-stricken faces. Flies swarmed and buzzed around the tableau of decaying bodies. The stink in the room caused Nellie to pinch her nose and scan the house, desperate to find the nearest exit.

"Shhh!" someone whispered, so noisily it might as well have been spoken aloud. "She's here! Get the tea!"

Nellie burst through the back door and took a deep breath. Behind the house, a prodigious patch of green grass underneath a sprawling willow tree provided the only bit of color in the blackened landscape that stretched out in all directions. On this rare stretch of grass sat a ridiculously long table, around which many mismatched but elegantly carved, tall-backed, formal chairs had been neatly arranged. In front of each, a place had been set on the pristine, white tablecloth. The plates, tea cups, and tiered serving plates were mismatched as well, but all were made of exquisite bone china. The table held a cacophony of half-eaten treats as well as tea pots of every shape and color. The carved chairs and tables were, at first glance, beautiful.

Upon closer scrutiny, Nellie noticed that the curvature of the legs of the table, and of the chair backs and arms, suggested the shapes of body parts: a feminine leg here and a muscular male arm there.

Most odd were the objects under the willow tree. Large, almost opaque, crystalline pods jutted from the ground, each one surrounded by smaller crystals that appeared to have grown out of the green grass. Nellie stepped closer and reached out to touch one.

To her surprise, something inside it moved. She pressed her face to the smooth surface and cupped her hands around her eyes to see inside. Folded up tightly inside she found a great, white rabbit whose body appendages had all been removed and sewn back on in the wrong places. Its torso moved as it breathed. Its head protruded from a shoulder socket, its pink nose twitched, and its blue eyes stared right back at Nellie. She gasped, and stepped back.

A purple crystalline pod near the rabbit's was broken open and surrounded by small shards. It leaked a viscous, dark-red fluid.

Another, greenish, pod, with red and white, polka-dot mushrooms surrounding its base, contained a colossal caterpillar with sharp, protruding fangs. Its green, yellow -spotted body undulated as it watched her through its milky-white eyes and used several of its many legs to push against its glass-like cocoon. Nellie stepped carefully past another shattered, brownish crystalline pod and advanced toward the table.

"Some of us have escaped, you see," a whisper floated musically toward Nellie. She glanced all about but couldn't find the source of the new voice. It was followed by a giggle, but the sound came from the other direction now. Nellie approached the table and touched the back of one of the empty chairs.

A tiny, muffled voice seemed to come from somewhere on the table top.

Twinkle, twinkle, great big cat!
Alice wonders where you're at.

Nellie tracked the sound to a bright-blue teapot covered in a black and white tea cozy. She lifted the lid, and the echoing little voice continued:

When you're gone you make me cry,
Oh please come back or I might die.
Twinkle, twinkle--

"There's no room! No room!" another voice cried, from somewhere close by. Nellie dropped the lid to the teapot and spun around.

"No room ..." echoed tall, bony, brown hare, as it hopped drunkenly toward the opposite side of the table. It wore clothes that, although originally finely tailored, were tattered and stained. The gruesomely gaunt hare dropped into a chair, kicked its long, thin back feet up on the table, and held aloft a wine glass brimming with a red liquid.

"I said NO ROOM!" The owner of the mysterious voice appeared suddenly, in Nellie's face, to roar the last two words, causing her to shriek and nearly fall backwards. He smiled, gently took her unsteady hand, and spun her around. "Well, look what the tabby cat dragged in!" he grinned, as pleasant as could be.

His dark clothing was dapper, yet over it he wore an apron fashioned from a type of leather that she couldn't identify. His top hat was constructed with upright metal bars, and inside the bars, his brain and other organic matter was trapped. The brim of the hat was so vast that it cast a shadow over his face, and Nellie could see only his red eyes and gleaming, wicked grin.

He sprung up. "Allow me to introduce myself. I am…" he gave a lengthy, sweeping bow," — your host!" He doffed his hat, leaving Nellie to gaze directly into the empty cavity where the top of his head should have resided.

Dr. Braun removed the sheet that had fed out of his machine and read the latest data feedback. He pulled his handkerchief out to dab at his increasingly sweaty brow.

"The Mad Hatter," he grimaced.

"It's happening again, isn't it?" Nurse Ball shot him an accusatory glare.

Conveniently ignoring her comment, he continued. "Alice may actually have found a way to infiltrate Dorothy's world through Nellie."

The color drained from Nurse Ball's face. "Does this mean she's still … alive down there somehow?"

Dr. Braun harrumphed. "Impossible! After all these years?"

His retort seemed, on its surface, to be a firm denial, yet his furrowed eyebrows and questioning tone left Nurse Ball feeling sick to her stomach.

Nellie was having difficulty deciding whether these two gruesome but quirky characters were a threat.

Keeping a healthy distance, she queried the peculiar man. "Dorothy mentioned a scarecrow. Is that you?"

He peered at Nellie from beneath the brim of his massive hat, and then broke into peals of screeching laughter. "Scarecrow? Buttons and billy goats — do I look like a scarecrow to you?"

Nellie took a deep breath and moved on. "Where's Dorothy?"

The macabre man jumped back and pointed his stylish walking stick at her. "Dorothy? Dorothy? Dorothy is lost. Oz belongs to us now!"

The giant hare at the table rolled its buggy eyes and thrust its sloshing goblet in the air. "To us! To us!"

"Who are you?"

The man spun around, his coattails following in a perfect arc, and presented his giant grin. "We come from a delightful place called Wonderland. We quite like it here though. Maybe we're going to stay."

"You can't stay here! This place doesn't belong to you."

In a flash, the man dashed toward Nellie and came to halt mere inches from her face. "And what are *you* going to *do* about it?" His red eyes glowed under the black hat like two burning coals in the dark, as his face drew closer and closer to hers.

Nellie shrank back, wide-eyed and frozen, lips trembling. The tip of his long, crooked nose touched hers. It felt cold and moist.

He suddenly threw back his head in another raucous fit of laughter. And, just as suddenly, he stopped and looked squarely at her. "Perhaps there is something you can do."

Nellie stared at him, unsure of whether to run or to stay and listen to the potentially fatal proposition.

The strange gent sauntered around the lawn, swinging his walking stick.

"You see, Nellie. We're here because we have nowhere to go. We've been exiled from our world. But you" — he pointed the walking stick at Nellie's stomach — "you can do something about it."

Nellie gritted her teeth. Yes, this man was dangerous and terrifying. But contrariwise, he was also aggravating, and he was wasting the time she could be using to find Dorothy.

"If you know where Dorothy is, tell me!" He continued on his roundabout stroll, toying with his walking stick. "If you want to be rid of us, you're going to have to free us." He turned back to her, and his eyes flashed.

"Break the mirror, Nellie."

"Break it and we can be free!" The brown hare leaned forward on the table and wiped its glistening lips on its sleeve.

"The mirror in the hallway?"

"Alice trapped us there."

Nellie blinked, thinking back to all that she had seen in the ornate looking glass. *We Are Here.*

"Alice? You know her too?"

Again, he burst into unhinged laughter. "Know her? She made us. We are part of her!"

Nellie shook her head. "I don't understand. None of this makes sense at all. Why me?"

The hare stood and pointed a brown paw at her. "Because you're the only one Alice can talk to."

"Alice!" squeaked the blue teapot.

"But why me? What's so special about me?"

"You?" the man took one lengthy stride toward her and twiddled the end of his walking stick at her. "There's nothing special about you. But ... someone else knows why. It's your secret."

He shoved her roughly toward the white crystalline pod and then began tapping on it. She looked from him to the pod with her eyebrows furrowed.

"Go on! She knows." The pod clinked with each tap of the walking stick.

Nellie leaned in and looked through the glass cocoon. Inside, the mutilated white rabbit looked back at her with its blues eyes, and blinked.

"The seed has been sown, but the rose has not yet begun to bloom," he whispered in her ear.

As his puzzling words took shape, she pulled away, aghast, and looked into his frightening, red eyes. "Are you trying to say that I'm pregnant? With Rose?"

"Tick, tock — now you're on time and using your noggin!" he patted the top of her head.

Her hands slid over her stomach as she tried to process the news.

"Tick, tock! Tick, tock!" the hare echoed, and took a swig from his goblet.

"But that can't be ..." she mumbled. "I haven't been with a man in over a year!"

"Messiahs like Alice need no men to be born. How else could you talk to the dead? Unless you are near death yourself?"

Nellie looked up suddenly. "So Alice is dead?"

He smiled. "Alice is Alice."

"And Dorothy?"

"Like two peas in a pod, those two are!" He began to walk and swing his walking stick again. "Same powers. Different worlds. Only" — he spun back to face her — "Dorothy's much more dangerous."

It was Nellie's turn to laugh this time. "Dorothy is a sweet girl!"

The man's screeching laughter silenced Nellie's. "Hardly. Alice created Wonderland out of curiosity and adventure. Dorothy created Oz from disaster and death."

"Oh Alice, my Alice!" piped the creature in the blue teapot.

"Her hands are covered in blood. Beware, Nellie, or you may meet the same fate as the witches."

"No," she shook her head. "You're wrong about her."

"Oh, am I? How well do you know your little fri —"

Suddenly, the man with his brains in a hat-cage and glowing red eyes began to back away from Nellie. He stared, wide-eyed, over Nellie's shoulder. The brown hare leapt up and tossed his goblet aside to snatch up a sharp, silver knife.

Nellie turned and exhaled with relief at the sight.

"Dorothy!"

Dorothy stood in front of the porch, but unlike Nellie, who smiled warmly, Dorothy looked strangely distant and cold. Out of the darkness behind her, three looming figures advanced and stood surrounding Dorothy. The monsters had returned, and Dorothy was surrounded by the tin man, the scarecrow, and the lion. The lion threw back its head to unleash a mighty roar, which was joined by the scarecrow's screech and the sound of the tin man's mechanical parts whirring into high gear. All three were chained together.

The man in the caged hat, and the cadaverous brown hare, crouched and hissed at Dorothy.

Dorothy lowered her face and glared at Alice's subjects. In a steely tone of voice, she commanded, "Leave this place, demons!"

. The man sneered. "You're still young in your powers. But if you're asking for a fight, I'd be happy to oblige!"

Large razor knives and wicked-looking scissors sprang from the palms of his hands. He gripped them firmly and grinned, advancing deliberately toward Dorothy and her minions.

The lion shook its mane and snarled, exposing extensive rows of shining sharp teeth. The tin man lowered his torso and braced for attack. The towering scarecrow seemed to grow even taller, extending his long arms in a spider-like fashion and emitting a blood-curdling screech.

Dorothy spoke, her eyes still locked with the man, "I will not fight except to defend my people."

"Maybe I can change your mind," he leered, light glinting from the deadly blades at his fingertips.

Dorothy turned to Nellie, "Nellie, run! I'll hold them off!"

Nellie wasted no time. She whirled around and ran back into the house.

"That's it Nellie! Run away. Don't worry about Rose. We'll look after her for you!" the strange man with the caged brains called after her.

Nellie paused for a moment in the doorway. "Just go!" Dorothy cried. Without wasting another moment, Nellie turned and ran back through the house, past the putrid piles of bodies, past the photographs, and toward the front door. With each flying step, she witnessed the walls, the ceiling, and the floor begin to contort as if someone were sticking a giant, invisible finger into the scenery and swirling it around like watercolors. A flash of bluish-white light filled the house, blinding Nellie, and she stumbled into the wall. The house, and the whole of Oz, rang out with the screams and shrieks of the demons, so shrill and powerful that Nellie felt as though her brain were being pierced by shards of crystal. She cried out, falling to her knees and plugging her ears tightly, vaguely aware that her eardrums might burst from the power of the unearthly keening.

On the table in the electrolysis room, white light flashed in Nellie's head, rocking her torso and limbs. Had the leather restraints not been so tight, the bucking of her body, caused by the massive jolts of electricity from the Dynamo machine, would have propelled her completely off of the table.

Dr. Braun watched the sparks fly from the electrodes on Nellie's head as it slammed into the table again and again. He did not flinch, even with the full understanding that each jolt must feel like ten thousand razor blades slicing into her flesh all at once.

"Alright," Dr. Braun nodded. "That should be enough. Power it down."

An orderly yanked the massive levers and switches on the Dynamo downward, causing the machine's high-pitched whirring to slow and then grind to a halt.

Nellie struggled to open her eyes. Lights all around her blinked like strobes — a result of her synapses firing and causing points of flashing blue light to pop in and out of her visual field. Yet, through it all, she could see the shape of little Rose floating above her. Her brown curls, her angelic face … but something was very wrong. She vibrated at an impossible speed, so fast that her head became a mere blur to Nellie.

Even though the machine was powering down, the shocks continued to zap Nellie. With each convulsion that wracked her body with pain and caused her back to arch against her will, she felt as through something like wings flapped beneath her back. She did not even begin to understand what this feeling was, but it filled her with primal terror. Nellie looked to the orderlies, to Nurse Ball, and to Dr. Braun. Each was looking right past what was happening. Her belly twisted and rolled, jutting this way and that to the sound of a deafening roar.

Nellie watched in horror, certain that something would push its way out of her stomach at any second, as the corporeal form of a little girl continued to float above her in amid the array of lights.

"MOMMY, NO! HELP ME! ALICE WANTS TO HURT ME!" the little girl screamed.

Dr. Braun glanced up, over the top of his spectacles. "Did you hear something?"

Each staff member in the room shook his or her head in reply.

"Hmm …" The doctor returned to finishing his record of the successful results in his notebook, dotting the period of his last sentence with solid stab at the paper. "She's stable. Good. Let's wrap this up for tonight. Take the patients to their rooms."

"We can still end this …" Nurse Ball's lowered tone was barely audible, but her glare spoke volumes.

"Why nurse, there is but one more phase to go and their treatment will be complete." He turned, and with a click of his heels, exited the room and left the staff to clean up.

With one final jolt, the Dynamo gave in and powered down completely. Nellie arched, with a final spasm, and collapsed into sweet unconsciousness.

CHAPTER 19

Nellie's mind drifted back to consciousness, yet she kept her eyes closed. If she opened them, she might be standing on a yellow brick road or in a long dark corridor, or perhaps floating in a watery tank or sitting on the cold wet floor of a cement wash room. Maybe this time it would be a gurney with leather straps aside a terrifying mechanical device or, best case scenario, the cold rock-hard cot in her room in the middle of a sanitarium.

She peeked through the slit of one eye — none of the above. This looked like the Seclusion Room in the very early morning. And, to her great surprise, she was no longer restrained. She slowly brought herself to a sitting position and took a general assessment of her being: bandaged leg to cover the cuts on her calf, freshly re-stitched cut over her eyebrow. Every muscle in her body ached, particularly in her back. Her skin was sore all over and covered in random purple and green bruises. And, most of all, she was so hungry and weak that she didn't know if she could pull herself off the bed to stand up and move.

Nellie groggily surveyed the room. There was another pleasant surprise to accompany her freedom. A white plate sat on the side table next to the bed with a simple but generous meal consisting of a peanut butter and jam sandwich, a big red apple, and a cup of milk. She nearly wept, such was her relief. The sandwich didn't even last a full five minutes, and the apple and milk were consumed so completely, that all that remained were the seeds and an empty cup.

Weariness flooded through her. With a full stomach, she slid her legs back under the thin blanket and gratefully, for the first time since her arrival at Bedlam, fell soundly and comfortably asleep before her head even touched the mattress.

Hours later, Nellie awoke to the sound of rustling paper. Nurse Ball was moving about the room, setting down some medication on a tin tray, along with more crayons and paper. "Time to take your next dose, Nellie."

"What am I doing here? What happened to my room?" Nellie asked, sitting up and stretching.

"Right now, you're susceptible to the slightest suggestion. We cannot have you mingling with the other patients until you've finished the final phase of your treatments."

"Nurse, where's Dorothy?"

"Instead of worrying about her, why don't you focus on your own recovery? Here." Nurse Ball tipped the small, white paper cup into the palm of Nellie's hand and two round, blue pills fell out. Nellie obligingly dropped them into her mouth and swallowed.

"Let me see." The nurse held Nellie's chin up and checked her mouth. Nellie lifted her tongue.

"Good girl." Nurse Ball nodded. "I noticed you lost your crayons and paper. Here're more for you." She glided over to the door and stopped. Turning back toward Nellie, she added, "I took the liberty of checking your records. Nellie Bly ... reporter for the New York Tribune."

Nellie's eyes popped open wide. The jig was up — but how?

In a soft voice, Nurse Ball looked directly into Nellie's eyes and said, "To find Alice, look under 'L' for 'Liddell.'"

CLANK!

The nurse's keys fell to the floor of the room as she stepped out the door and shut it behind her.

Dorothy lay on her hard cot in her locked room, her body completely inert from the latest round of drugs that the doctor had ordered. At the sound of a key scraping in the lock, she forced one eye open.

Dr. Braun propped her door open. She watched him

through blurry, medicated eyes as he stood up, disappeared around the corner for a moment, and then reappeared, pushing a squeaky utility cart that contained an unfamiliar device.

"What are you doing?" she heard herself ask out loud, but, with her tongue feeling three feet thick, her voice sounded like that of a stranger.

"This, my dear, is what I like to call the Cognome Machine." He positioned the cart next to her cot and picked up a strange headset fashioned of leather straps and metal wires. He connected it to her head and pulled up a stool so he could sit in front of her.

"Now, Dorothy. I want you to help me test this out. I want you to focus. Focus your thoughts and your dreams into this screen."

He flipped a metal switch, and the screen sprang to life, glowing with black and white specks that jumped about like a salt-and-pepper snowstorm. Dorothy stared into the luminous display, unable to look at anything else.

"Share your thoughts with me. So I can share them with you … ."

As Dorothy stared groggily at the glowing screen, as if by magic, the black and white specks jumped frenetically until an image began to form.

Dr. Braun smiled as the familiar picture took shape — a sunlit farm surrounded by swaying grass and flocks of animals. Under a tree, fuzzy ducklings waddled unsteadily after their mother. "Fascinating!" he breathed, reaching out to touch the images moving across the screen. "Is there anything out beyond the farm? A forest, perhaps?" Just as his fingertips made contact with the glass, the images disappeared and the monitor displayed the jumping white and black specks once more. Dorothy was too mesmerized by the light of the screen to do anything but stare slack-jawed at it.

He gently removed the headset from Dorothy's head and shut off the machine with the silver toggle. "You are making remarkable progress, Dorothy." He roughly patted her shoulder. He packed up his odd machine and smiled, talking to Dorothy regardless of her ability to comprehend him. "Not even Alice made it this far!"

He stood and rolled the cart out of the room, shutting the door behind him. The lock engaged, and Dorothy heard the doctor's soft chuckling grow more distant as he wheeled the cart away down the hall.

"I am not Alice..." she whispered.

In the depths of Bedlam, the vault door loomed in the flickering light of the old light bulb.

"Dorothy ..." a gravelly voice whispered.

The door shook, dislodging small showers of dirt that rained from the ceiling and clouded the corridor.

After a quiet dinner and some time spent writing with her crayons and paper, Nellie got up and pulled the nurse's keys out from under the mattress. The familiar sounds of lockdown echoed in the halls as Bedlam's staff noisily secured the many doors and snapped the main switches to douse banks of lights.

She waited patiently. Tonight, thanks to Nurse Ball, getting out of her room would be much easier than it had been when she had employed the hairpins. When the staff had been safely out of the halls for a while, and the sounds of snoring filled the asylum, Nellie got out and tiptoed to Dr. Braun's office. His office was dark and locked. Checking to make sure that no one approached, she slid each key into the office door's lock. After several tries, the lock clicked, and she turned the doorknob.

Dr. Braun's office was odd at best, even during daylight hours. Now she beheld it at night, when the creatures in the jars and the photographs of the doctor's inventions were at their most unsettling. This time, however, she knew where she needed to go. With keys in hand, in no time at all Nellie had unlocked the doctor's file cabinet and was thumbing through his files. "'L' for 'Liddell'," she mumbled, flipping through the hanging manila folders one by one.

GHBEISH. MOORE. TEO. JOHNSTON. LOPEZ. WHITE. HUPMAN.She flipped frantically back and forth through the files until ...

LIDDELL.

This was it.

She pulled the folder out, locked the cabinet, and scurried over to sit in a patch of moonlight that shone through the window. She flopped the file open.

Here was a photograph of Alice. It was the same photograph that hung on the wall of the Teahouse in Oz. A petite, beautiful young girl, innocent and happy, sitting under a tree and petting the pleased, gray tabby cat that curled up on the white apron of her dress. She was still too far away for Nellie to see her face clearly, but this child differed markedly from the horror that now bore her visage.

The first of Dr. Braun's notes was clipped to the right side of the folder:

I first met Alice in 1911. She was a severely troubled child, but gifted with tremendous psychic powers.

CHAPTER 20

The pale young girl sat in a dark corner of the room, unmoving.

"Yes, Dr. Braun," a young woman in dress similar to the young girl's spoke in hushed tones with one of Bedlam Asylum's newer doctors. "I am her legal guardian. Sister, to be exact. My name is Edith Liddell."

"Miss Liddell, if I may enquire," Dr. Braun smoothed back his wavy black hair. "What is it about her imaginary friends that bother you so? A friendly rabbit in a waistcoat seems like a perfectly acceptable imaginary companion that she will most likely outgrow when the time is right."

Edith's face flushed. She cast a quick sideways glance toward the girl in the shadows and leaned toward the doctor.

"Em ... it's, well ... em ... they're not normal imaginary friends, you see. She describes these ... these creatures that ... well, they just sound absolutely ... mad. There's a cat with glowing eyes that speaks utter nonsense and then just disappears. Well, all of it except its smile disappears. There are things to eat that make things grow big and small, and bottles of medicine that one can swallow to grow a snake-like neck. And there's a man who has gone insane, the Mad Hatter I think he is. And, worst of all, there's a Queen of Hearts who wants nothing more than to ..." she leaned toward the doctor to whisper in his ear.

"Cut off your head!" the little girl in the corner finished, in a hushed tone.

Edith raised her eyebrows and nodded.

Dr. Braun nodded and jotted some notes on Alice's file.

She was born in Oxford. Origins of her parents were unknown. She had one sister, named Edith, who committed her.

Alice was brought here because of night terrors — of a place she called Wonderland. But nightmares were not what made her special.

Alice sat in the common room with her favorite red and white chess set, a piece of drawing charcoal, and a small stack of paper. The picture in front of her depicted a tabby cat with an ear-to-ear grin and rolling, yellow eyes, floating in a tree at a fork in the road.

Behind Alice's chair, a group of patients gathered and whispered. Their words were unkind, and their plans were to be cruel to her.

Alice spun around in her chair and glared at them. They instantly dispersed without another word. Only one inmate remained and stood her ground, returning Alice's glare.

She was attuned to the negative emotions of other people. She could read thoughts. The inmates were all terrified of her.

Alice stood and approached the woman. She walked directly over to stand toe-to-toe with her, never breaking the stare, never blinking. The woman's lip curled into a smirk as she looked down at the girl's lanky, pale, blond hair hanging in her face. She put her fingers on Alice's shoulders and gave her a rough shove. Alice stumbled back a few steps, but she recovered and stood her ground and clenched her fists at her sides.

Suddenly, the woman fell to her knees, grasping at her ears and wailing for help. Blood dribbled from her ears and spattered her gray gown as she scratched at her eyes.

Dr. Braun and a nurse entered the room as Alice padded quietly away from the woman, who was writhing on the ground in anguish. The nurse ran to the bleeding patient, but the doctor stood motionless, trying to assess what had happened.

When I first witnessed a psychic attack on an inmate by Alice, I did not understand what was before my very eyes. Yet the strange coincidences became too many to be written off as pure imagination. The staff began to talk. The patients took great pains to stay as far away from Alice as they could manage. It was not long before I reached the conclusion that this girl had a special gift, and the responsibility to explore the science and source of it rested solely upon my shoulders. This was the genesis of Project: Alice.

I designed and developed three special programs to control Alice's hypnotic powers. The first induction room was the Sensory Deprivation Tank. I experimented with sound, light, sleep, drugs, and every method of therapeutic treatment within my power to address mental instability. Having to explore unheard of abilities, this was all I could grasp at to try to determine the cause of her gifts. It took many weeks of careful scrutiny, but eventually it became evident that Alice's greatest potential could be achieved when the conditions were set in low lighting.

Alice lay in the saline solution, floating peacefully in the dark as she dreamt. Dr. Braun and Nurse Ball stood in the Observation room, monitoring the young girl's vital signs and making notes regarding the conditions of the treatment.

Alice twitched, her long blond hair floating out around her in the eerie quiet of the tank.

"Nooooo... "the little girl moaned, her eyes moving rapidly left and right beneath her eyelids. "I won't! I won't!" she cried from another place in her dreams.

Nurse Ball gripped Dr. Braun's wrist tightly. He looked up at her to exclaim his dissatisfaction at having his penmanship ruined unnecessarily, but the sight of a stool, which was rising up off the cement floor, took the words out of his mouth. Light bulbs all around the room popped and shattered one by one as the doctor and the nurse ran to the tank to free Alice from her nightmare.

We started by recreating the conditions of the first hypnotic induction. For this new experiment I created a machine. A mechanical tube was constructed housing a hard vacuum.

Alice lay strapped to a metal bed. Her rosy cheeks had turned chalky; her eyes had become sunken and tired. She wore a leather strap over her head, and a bite guard kept her mouth immobile.

Dr. Braun flipped a switch on the early version of his electrolysis machine, and instantly Alice's face contorted with pain. She did not cry out, but instead made efforts to give as little feedback from the shocking volts as possible.

In this next experiment I introduce electricity into the brain, to eliminate any neurological inconsistencies. I also created a device capable of capturing brain wave patterns and interpreting them into light. This I labeled the Cognome Machine.

The Cognome Machine built from the vacuum tube device housed a phosphor-coated screen. This screen is bombarded with electrons creating an image of the patients thoughts, similar to the way in which Alice uses her powers to project her thoughts into the minds of the other inmates..

Dr. Braun tapped his pen against the paper and looked hard at the now sickly girl in the chair before him. She wore the headset that connected her, by metal wires, to the screen filled with white light. All she could do is blink and squint in her best efforts not to see the light. Dr. Braun yanked the headset from young Alice, tossed it to the machine, and stormed from the room.

After testing her thoroughly, I had to admit that Alice had made little to no progress. What I came to find out later was that Alice was purposely failing the tests.

Alice stood in her room with her back to the door. She held her arms out from her sides, her treasured caterpillar locket in one hand and her teddy bear in the other. Dr. Braun watched through the observation window as the teddy bear and the locket lifted from her hands and began to rotate around her in midair. The locket revolved in a gradual orbit about her until it reached the space in front of her eyes, where the lid flipped open and allowed Alice to see Dr. Braun studying her through the window. The doctor shuddered; Alice glared at him in the reflection of the locket, those sickly, yellow eyes focused on him with concentrated hatred.

He stepped backward into the shadows and left. With each step he took, his strides became longer and faster.

"Dr. Braun? Is everything alright?" Nurse Ball called out to the man she saw bolting down the hall.

She was playing me for the fool. Mocking me. Project: Alice was a success, but she had misled me into believing I was a failure. I took matters into my own hands.

The wan young girl pulled and fought against the doctor's grip on her wrist as he strode toward a door marked "Hypnotic Induction 3." She braced her bare heels on the floor to keep from passing the threshold, but Dr. Braun's impatience won the match; he yanked her arm cruelly, pulling her so hard that she flew headfirst through the doorway and pitched forward into a metal door.

Alice moaned and fell to her knees, holding her mouth, with tears spilling down her cheeks. She pulled her hand away and found it stained pink and red from the blood that poured from her lacerated lip and tongue. Her front teeth were chipped and broken.

Dr. Braun locked the door. "Get up." He opened the metal door, which Alice's fall had dented slightly. It was the door to a capsule-shaped apparatus in the center of the room.

"Please …" she cried from the floor, hiccupping, as blood ran down her chin. "Please, no more … ."

"Get up, I said." He pulled her up by the wrist and pushed her into the seat in the capsule.

I decided to push the experiment forward. Alice was taken to the third and final hypnotic induction room. After this test, I would have what I needed to finish my machine.

Dr. Braun circled the capsule, flipping toggles on the control panel, which brought power to the machine. Inside the capsule, Alice looked up at a circle of pulsing light. The circle spun faster and faster, the light flickering more and more. Her eyes grew wide.

Once the subject is broken down and the neural patterns reset, he or she becomes highly susceptible to outside suggestion. The Cognome Machine operates in much the same way as the Saturation Chambers. By

beaming images back at the subject, we can achieve
total mind control. Total obedience.

Decades of research on hypnosis now can come
together into one little machine: the Cognome Machine.

Alice sat on her cot in her room, holding her teddy
bear in her weak, thin, pale arms. Dr. Braun's Cognome
Machine rested on the cart in front of her, and a headset
connected her to the device.

"Alice, I know you can do this." Dr. Braun insisted,
with an edge in his voice. "Look at the light. You can
show me Wonderland — you've done it before."

Alice stared blankly into the light, with glassy eyes.
But nothing on the screen changed; no pictures took
shape.

But with Alice, the connection was incomplete. She
fought the experiments, and measures had to be taken.
The only method left to stimulate the patient to reach
her maximum potential had to be to release the pressure
on her brain. Methods for achieving this are well

documented, but these unorthodox treatments were not prescribed by Western medicine.

Alice sat strapped to a medical chair, this time in a surgical room. The only other person in the sterile, white room was Dr. Braun, who was busy laying out tools and an anesthetic on a metal tray. He wore a surgical beanie and gloves.

"Don't you worry about a thing, Alice." He patted the shoulder of the wide-eyed girl, ignoring the tears that rolled down both cheeks and the muffled protests that were lost behind the cloth tied around her head between her broken teeth. He leaned over her to make minor adjustments to the long screws of the metal restraint which, like a cage, held her head completely immobile. With a black pen, he made precise measurements and marks in the center of the top of her forehead.

"This will be over before you know it." He picked up a syringe and held it in front of him, pushing the air out of the glass so that only the liquid remained in the receptacle.

Alice squeezed her eyes shut and concentrated as hard as she possibly could on the lights above her, the terror flowing through her like never before.

The light began to flicker. Dr. Braun paid no attention and went about his work as, for him, this had become par for the course.

The light went out, and Alice had it —she had the darkness she needed. She drew the picture in her mind's eye: beneath a vast willow tree sat the long table with all of her friends. Here was the Mad Hatter, with his velvet coat and tall top hat. Come to me, friend. Here was the Cheshire Cat, with his rolling, yellow eyes and broad, white grin. He will save me. Come to me, my mad March Hare and my sweet Dormouse! Oh, White Rabbit! Oh, Queen of Hearts!

The remaining lights in the room began to flicker on and off. Dr. Braun moved the tray closer to Alice's chair and brought the syringe to her arm. "You're going to fall asleep now… "

"Hatter! Cheshire Cat!" her muffled screams pushed through the cloth gag.

"... and when you wake up, you'll feel so much better."

The wall behind Dr. Braun warped. He touched the syringe to Alice's arm.

In a blinding flash of light, the Mad Hatter stepped into the room, wearing his purple, velvet coat and top hat and swinging his walking stick. Fast on his heels jumped the Cheshire Cat, a giant long lean silky tabby with golden eyes and a playful grin.

Dr. Braun pushed the needle into Alice's small arm, and instantly the room began to swim before her eyes.

"What-what, my dear girl?" The colorful Mad Hatter skipped to her side.

The Cheshire Cat put his white-tipped paws up on the edge of the chair arm and folded them over each other. "Which way did you mean for us to go? This way or that?" he purred, and grinned.

Dr. Braun could not see or hear the visitors in the room with them. He picked up a hand-operated drill.

"Stop him ... ." Alice whispered, as the room began to shrink to a pinpoint.

The doctor inserted the drill into an aperture of the metal restraint cage, and gently placed the point on the black mark he had etched on her forehead. The aperture held the conical point perfectly perpendicular to her skull.

"What did you say?" the Mad Hatter leaned his ear down to her moving lips.

Dr. Braun cranked the hand drill with speed and precision. The drill bit entered Alice's forehead and carved a hole the size of a dime into her skull, the drill point slowing as the tip met with bone. Sweat trickled from his brow, his efforts doubling with the difficulty of turning the drill tip through solid bone.

POP!

With the sickening sound of release, Alice felt a rushing, a gushing, and a warm wetness pouring from her forehead onto her neck and shoulders. Dr. Braun grabbed several sterile cloths to keep the blood that spurted, fountain-like, from her cranium to a minimum.

The world was changing before her dazed eyes. She began to sink. As she sank, the colors disappeared. Reality seeped into her dear Wonderland. Before her eyes, her childhood seeped away and the Mad Hatter grew dark. His clothes turned to black; his apron changed to leather. His face disappeared into shadow, and his eyes turned from bright green and brown to blood red.

The Cheshire Cat at her side stopped grinning. His eyes filled with black liquid, his fur fell out in clumps, and his perfect, white teeth dripped with molten metal that began to form perfect, deadly points.

"There, now. You should feel so much better. Your mind is now open." Dr. Braun patted her shoulder. "I believe we've exorcized your demons."

Alice struggled to stay awake, but lost the fight. As she slipped into unconsciousness, the Mad Hatter and the Cheshire Cat vanished.

In a room somewhere on the sixth floor, Dr. Braun unlocked Alice's hidden room and wheeled the

Cognome Machine in. This time, the headset had been removed and in its place was a small, yellow plug, about the size of a dime.

Alice sat on her bed, staring at the wall. The teddy bear on her pillow and her favorite red and white chess set remained untouched. Her eyes were yellow, her teeth broken, her lips split from dehydration and stained with blood. Her hair hung in her face, unwashed and un-brushed.

"And how are we today, Alice?" Dr. Braun rolled his cart in and threw a metal stool down in front of her with a thunk.

Alice did not answer.

"It's time to try the next phase of your treatment, Alice — time to try the Cognome Machine again. Here we go."

He grasped the yellow plug, its metal tip now exposed, and gently pushed it into the hole in Alice's forehead, breaking open the skin that had started to form a healing barrier over the wound.

"Now I want you to think about Wonderland, Alice. Think about the Mad Hatter for me. Show me the Mad Hatter."

With this simple device, we can make people think anything we want. We can make them feel anything we want.

Dr. Braun watched the flickering screen expectantly, his pen and paper at hand, ready to record notes. The screen did not change, and Alice did not move. Her glassy eyes wandered toward the shadows in the corner.

"No!" Dr. Braun grabbed her chin and roughly forced her head back toward the bright screen. "I said show me Wonderland!"

She did not answer him, and the screen continued to flicker with white and black specs.

Dr. Braun stood up, no longer able to contain his rage. "We have NOT worked so hard and for so long for you just to give up now, Alice! I said SHOW ME WONDERLAND!"

He slapped her across the face to snap her out of her stupor.

And then ... everything fell apart.

Alice's head snapped toward Dr. Braun and she looked into his eyes with a rage he had never seen before. She flew to her feet, an invisible wind blowing her hair, whipping it above and all around her head and shoulders.

BOOM!

Dr. Braun's body flew back against the wall, and the door to her chamber blew outward off its hinges. Alice walked out of the room, down the hall, and down the stairs toward the sounds of Bedlam staff member shouting and the patient howling and running in circles.

Alice had had enough.

Dr. Braun came to, sprang to his feet, and raced out the door to the stairs, taking them two by two.

What I saw next chilled me to the bone.

The walls downstairs were charred as if a massive fire ball had just rolled through the halls. Orderlies and inmates raced around, in a state of utter pandemonium, in search of shelter.

Alice walked slowly down the center of the corridor, and, with each step, flames sprang up the walls around her. Any persons who were unfortunate enough to be too close to Alice's swath of destruction fell to their knees, grabbed at their ears and pulled at their eyes, screaming.

Everywhere she went, she left a path of devastation. She was set on revenge.

Behind Alice, the still struggling bodies of inmates and orderlies burst into flame, quickly transforming into blackened husks. Two nurses, armed with syringes, ran toward Alice, but they were not able to get close enough to subdue her before they fell to the floor with searing pain in their eyes and ears.

At the entryway, Alice stopped. She stood in front of the ornate looking glass, staring at her reflection. Her eyes grew wide and her mouth fell open. She rushed toward the mirror, screaming, and hammered at the glass surface with her small clenched fists. The glass splintered.

For some reason, Alice reacted very strongly when she saw the mirror. It was as if she had never seen the horror of who she was until that moment. But this gave us an advantage ...

An orderly saw his opportunity and took it, quickly closing the distance to Alice and stabbing her in the neck with a full dose of sedative. Alice cried out, and the orderly flew backward into a stair railing. She turned around and, with staring, yellow eyes full of hatred, she approached him. He got to his knees but could not move any further, the pressure and pain building in his head with each passing second. He screamed, clutching his head between his palms. And, as Alice stopped in front of him, his eyes rolled up under his eyelids, and his cranium burst. Chunks of bloody brain matter splattered both the walls and Alice.

But his sacrifice was not in vain. Her eyes blurred and her vision swam. She dropped to her knees and weakly yanked the empty syringe from her neck. Struggling to get her feet underneath her and rise to walk, she lost all feeling in her legs and collapsed to the floor.

· *I was never able to explain what I saw next. It defied all scientific logic. But somehow, the mirror saved us.*

The small, badly bruised girl lay sprawled on the floor, eyelids fluttering, and the flames throughout the halls and rooms of Bedlam Asylum immediately abated. A swirling, black mist spiraled up from her body, with solid bits of black matter churning in the center. As if suddenly magnetized, the black smoke shot toward the mirror and seeped into the crack in the glass.

When the last of the smoke had disappeared into the mirror, Alice fell unconscious. The cracks in the mirror sealed up; the glass healed. Within moments, the mirror had become, once again, nothing but an elegant decorative piece there to adorn the wall.

A shaken Dr. Braun stood beside the weeping Nurse Ball amid the carnage, as they numbly surveyed what was left of Bedlam Asylum.

Alice's heavily medicated body sat strapped in a chair that was connected to a plethora of tubes and wires. The chair was carried into the center of an empty vault by a group of orderlies.

We locked her in a vault deep below the basement of the asylum. Here she would be imprisoned behind steel walls lined with lead to inhibit her psychic abilities.

There she will stay. Along with any hopes of my research ever becoming a success.

CHAPTER 21

D r. Braun sat in the chair he had pulled up beside a gurney. The woman in the gurney lay inert, covered by a pristine, white blanket. Drip by drip, fluid traveled down rubber tubing and entered her body via the intravenous needle that had been carefully inserted into and taped to the back of her hand.

She was an older woman. Her long, silver hair lay neatly arranged on the pillow; her wrinkled, pale skin and soft pink cheeks were the very picture of peaceful slumber.

A tear rolled down his cheek as he held her papery, weathered hand in his, motionless and limp.

"I have failed you again," he whispered, and laid his head down on the white blanket.

She smiled and knelt down to be at the same level as the small boy, who laughed and held his pudgy hands and arms out to her. She smoothed his black curls and kissed his forehead, and he ran into her arms to squeeze her as tightly as his small arms could manage.

"Mama," he whispered, and laid his head on her shoulder.

She turned the oil lamp down, the room dark now except for the dim light from the dying fire. She scooped the child up and moved over to the rocking chair in front of the fireplace's soft, blue flames. She rocked the small boy back and forth and hummed softly in his ear.

He wrapped her long, silky black hair around his dimpled fingers and then stroked it back down to shiny smoothness again, a sigh upon his pink lips. "Tell me the story again."

"Oh, you want to hear the story about the queen and her magic mirror?" she laughed.

"Yes, and the cottage in the forest with the little beds and the little dishes." He smiled, again twirling her hair round and round.

"Oh, Henry, do you never tire of that same old story?"

The little boy sat up in her lap to look into her face. "No, it is my favorite!" he exclaimed.

"Very well, then." She pulled his head back down to rest on her shoulder, and gently rocked back and forth.

"Once upon a time, there was a beautiful queen. She sat sewing in her favorite chair by the window, and watched the snow fall while she stitched. The queen pricked her fingertip on the sewing needle, and three drops of blood fell onto the white snow that lay on the ebony window ledge. She looked at the red and the white and said, 'Oh, how I wish that I had a daughter who had skin as white as snow, lips as red as blood,

and hair as black as the wood of the window frame!'
And do you know what happened next?"

"She had a little baby girl!" the boy exclaimed,
with a triumphant grin. "Snow White!"

"That's right. She named her baby Snow White."

She rocked back and forth before the warm fire —
swish, swish, swish, swish — and whispered her son's
favorite bedtime tale into his ear.

Swish, swish — the warmth of the fire felt so lovely.
Swish, swish.

"Tell me of their little dishes," the boy said through
his fingertips, which he sucked on as he drowsed on her
shoulder.

"Why don't I just show you instead?" she smiled,
smoothing his hair down and resting her head on his.
She reached out and slid a small, gold hand mirror into
his fingers. He looked into its surface, but instead of the
reflection of their faces, the mirror showed a scene of a
cottage in a forest. He stared at the image, sleepy and
cozy in his mother's arms.

Suddenly, in the mirror, the little boy saw his

mommy on the dirt path in the midst of the great, green forest filled with towering trees. His eyes grew wide with wonder. Blue birds flitted between the tree tops. Leaves fluttered and spun to the forest floor through rays of sunshine that passed through the shadow to light the woodland path.

"Come, Henry," she grinned and held her fingertips out to him. "Let's go see their little beds!"

He squealed with delight, holding his hands over his mouth lest he burst with joy. Henry dashed forward to grab his mother's hand, and together they ran toward the small thatched cottage at the end of the path.

Both the path and the cottage walls were lined with colorful flowers as well as minuscule benches that were hand carved from logs. The short, white door to the cottage was only slightly larger than Henry himself. He held his breath and reached out to touch the doorknob.

"No, Henry. Always knock first." His mother grasped the tiny door knocker between her thumb and forefinger, and gently sounded a tap-tap-tap on the front door.

They listened and waited for an answer, but none came. He looked up at her questioningly.

"Very well," she nodded.

He carefully turned the knob, and the small door swung open. The cottage was everything Henry had dreamt it could be. The kitchen in the corner had a wooden sink stacked with clean, drying dishes and cups that were just Henry's size. In front of the sink was a long wooden table with benches and, oddly, eight place settings. Henry looked up to his mother, with the question upon his lips, but he could see, by the way that her eyes softened and her lips quivered, that the eighth place setting remained ready for her infrequent visits.

Henry tugged at her hand to pull her into the living area and in front of the fireplace. A set of various pipes lined the mantel, cleaned and ready, and next to them was a leather pouch. Stools and soft cushions surrounded the fireplace — this must be where the cottage's inhabitants gather after dinner to warm themselves before the fire. Henry flopped down on one of the large cushions and fell backward to grin at the candle-lined chandelier that hung above them. His mother sat down next to him and pulled a small basket toward her. It was filled with shiny red apples.

"What is that, mama?"

"There's a note. Perhaps they left it for us?" She picked up a piece of paper from inside the basket and read its contents aloud, "A gift for the fairest of them all." She plucked an apple from the top of the pile and polished it on her skirt.

"Who's it from, mama?" Henry picked up the piece of paper and puzzled at the sweeping, black calligraphy.

"I would think it was left here for you and me!" She smiled and touched her fingertip to his nose. She bit into the apple's crisp red skin.

"But mama, what if it —" the boy began.

His mother's face suddenly drained of all color; her eyes widened. The apple rolled out of her hand onto the floor before him and Henry could see that, where the apple's interior should have been a creamy white, instead it was black. When he reached out to touch it, the apple bubbled, hissed, and melted away before his eyes.

"Mama!" he cried out, scrambling to her.

She gaped at him, shaking her head and grasping at her throat, unable to draw breath. He put his fingers against her face and his fingertips into her mouth, trying to find the piece of apple.

She pulled him close, held him still in her arms, and closed her eyes.

"MAMA! MAMA!" he cried, tears spilling, trying to pull away to help her somehow. Her body went limp and she fell to the cushions. He put his small hands on her shoulders and shook her, trying to sit her up again. Her face looked strangely peaceful through his blurry, tear-filled eyes. He knelt next to her and wiped his vision clear with his sleeve.

She was still alive. Henry's mouth fell open and he reached out, with shaking fingertips, to touch her face. It was warm. Her cheeks and lips were still red.

In a bright, white flash, Henry was, once again, home in his mother's arms in the rocking chair.

"Mama!" he sat up and grasped her shoulders. The small, gold hand mirror clunked to the rug.

Her head rested against the rocking chair back as she dozed, her chest rising and falling with the shallow breaths of deep sleep.

No matter how hard he shook her, pled with her, or touched her face, she would not open her eyes.

"Mama ..." Dr. Braun murmured into his arm on the white blanket. The sound of his own voice startled him awake. He lifted his head and rubbed at his bleary eyes. His surroundings came into focus. The darkness in the white room meant it was still the middle of the night. He slid open the drawer of the nightstand and pulled out the small, gold hand mirror. Taking his mother's hand again, he looked into the mirror.

There was the glass coffin on the dais in the middle of the forest, just as it had been for decades. Inside of it lay his mother — her raven hair, her red-rose cheeks — asleep for all eternity. Standing solemnly next to the glass coffin was the same small, gray-haired man who had built it. His small hat hung from his hands as he stood near the head of the dais, his head hung in reverence.

Dr. Braun murmured the same words of frustration he had repeated time and time again to the mirror, for years on end. "If only I could just communicate with you, I know you could help her ... ."

He let go of his mother's hand, and the image in the mirror vanished. He slid it back into the drawer.

"There's hope, Mama," he whispered. "I'm going to go and try again now."

Before he would step outside to lock the door to which only he and Nurse Ball had keys, he kissed the sleeping woman's forehead, his lips grazing the small round dime-sized scar in the middle.

Nellie fell back into the chair behind Dr. Braun's desk, stunned. Alice had caused the burnt, peeling paint in the Fantasyland wing. Alice had gone insane because Dr. Braun wanted to find a way to see into Wonderland, perhaps even to control it or to enter it somehow. And Alice had been locked in the vault for ... how long?

The date on the final entry of the chart was 1912.

Ten years. Alice had been locked away in the vault for ten years. None of *this* made sense; Nellie glanced up to the chalkboard and scanned the formulas and scribbles for something that might. Her hand jumped to her mouth.

The faint chalk remnants left the ghost of the word "Alice" on the blackboard. Over it in white chalk, two words had been written in a strong hand:

PROJECT: DOROTHY

The door to the Saturation Chamber swung open, and Dr. Braun, propelled by new energy and determination, ushered Dorothy over the threshold. A nearby orderly flipped the power switches, readying the machine.

"Is it going to hurt?" The sleepy girl rubbed at her eyes and flumped onto the chamber's seat.

"This is the last part of the treatment, Dorothy." Dr. Braun smiled, patted her shoulder, and shut the chamber door. Dorothy sat straight up and peered out at him through the small porthole. Now that a door was involved in locking her into something, alarm was setting in.

"It won't hurt at all," he replied, through the glass. "It's like the pictures on the screen. You just have to concentrate on them."

"What kind of pictures?"

"All the good memories of your Aunt Em and Uncle Henry."

Dorothy nodded and retreated warily back into the machine.

With a hum, the apparatus came to life, and Dr. Braun slipped a pair of goggles over his eyes.

Nellie had long since left behind any notion of covering her tracks. Drawers hung open, files were everywhere, and papers lay strewn about as if a hurricane had blown through Dr. Braun's office.

"Come on ... where is it?" She rifled frantically through his desk drawers. Upon tearing open the bottom drawer of his desk, she found it — the file marked "BLY" in bold, red lettering.

She ripped the file open and looked to the stacked medical notes on the left. Her eyes filled with tears. Stamped in bold, green lettering on the most recent note was the confirmation she needed, yet still could not comprehend: pregnant. Her trembling hand went reflexively to her abdomen and she closed her eyes, listening and feeling for any sign of the tiny being named Rose.

The door to the office was swung open by the hand of an orderly who, in patrolling the halls, had noticed that the door hung ajar.

"HEY!" he yelled, pulling out his whistle.

Within moments, the sounds of whistles repeated up and down the halls of Bedlam, triggering the alarm. Nellie had nowhere to run.

CHAPTER 22

T he walls of the Saturation Chamber had only just begun to spin around Dorothy when the sound of the alarm issued through the halls, causing cries of distress from worried inmates in their cells.

Nervous from the sudden alarm, the orderly asked, "What's going on, Dr. Braun?"

He pulled the goggles off his eyes and stuck his head out into the hall. "I'm not sure. Wait here."

He took a step through the threshold, but the orderly grabbed his arm. "But what should I do?"

"Nothing. It'll be another ten minutes before the machine needs to be powered down."

A team of nurses and orderlies ran past the door, and Dr. Braun quickly followed.

The way out of the doctor's office was already being guarded by an orderly by the time that Dr. Braun and Nurse Ball came racing down the hall, from opposite directions. The doctor pushed his way through and into the office to find a wild-eyed Nellie scanning the room for an escape route.

"What are you doing in here?!" he shouted, red-faced. He spied the files in her hand and pointed a shaking finger, "Give those back RIGHT NOW!"

Nellie's eyes narrowed. She dropped the files and grabbed the edge of the rolling chalkboard that contained Dr. Braun's scribbled research.

"Don't you dare ..." he spoke through gritted teeth, glaring at her from beneath furrowed eyebrows.

With all her strength, Nellie shoved the chalkboard, hurling it across the room. The orderly and the doctor braced for impact and, in that split second of distraction, Nellie darted around the outskirts of their reach and through the door. Nurse Ball flattened against the wall to avoid collision with Nellie, who turned the corner of the threshold and sprinted down the hall.

"Why didn't you stop her?" Dr. Braun shouted.

"But doctor, "she began, hands outstretched.

"Don't you test me, Ms. Ball!" He jabbed a finger in the air toward her. He spun around to the orderly and added, "Activate the lockdown, now!" He strode back into the room and swept a clanking black mass of keys from the floor. Holding the key ring out before him, he jingled the keys at the head nurse, his eyebrows aloft.

"I ... must have dropped them." Nurse Ball cast her eyes down to the floor, her cheeks flushing.

"Is that why you let Nellie escape, too?"

She did not return his gaze, but stood with her hands folded.

"After today, you're fired!" he yelled, rage coursing through him. He hurled her key ring at the wall with such force that it dented the wall next to her head before clanging to the floor.

Inside the chamber, the walls spun round and round Dorothy, flooding her senses with a series of blinking images. Photographs of her uncle and aunt flashed before her: the two of them holding hands in front of the farmhouse, Aunt Em standing on the steps with a flower in her hair, Uncle Henry throwing a mound of hay to the top of a haystack with his pitchfork. The images spun faster and faster, beginning to blur together until Aunt Em stood in front of Uncle Henry with a flower in her hair, holding his hand, and a pitchfork lying at their feet.

Dorothy watched, slack-jawed, as the images moved. Aunt Em was no longer a still photograph; she let Uncle Henry's hand drop from hers and turned to face Dorothy. Uncle Henry in turn stooped to pick up the pitchfork and hold it, upright, next to him. Their eyes shone with white light.

"Welcome home, Dorothy," said Uncle Henry.

"Now we can finally be happy." Aunt Em smiled and looked to her husband.

Dorothy remained absolutely still, hypnotized by the images that filled her imagination.

The orderly fidgeted, glancing toward the door — still no sign of Dr. Braun. He leaned over to peek through the window of the chamber door. He gasped.

The girl's face was now bathed in an unnatural blue light whose source was not any of the doctor's machinery. It seemed to be emanating from the girl herself — from her eyes.

The alarm's incessant, shrill wail rent the night air in, and all around, Bedlam Island, as Nellie continued at breakneck speed through the halls to the entrance. She could see the tall doors just ahead, and the probability of escape propelled her aching limbs forward.

But, as she came skidding to a halt and reached for the doorknob, a massive iron plate dropped down over the door.

BAM!

Nellie's head swam and her stomach turned as she watched iron plates drop, one by one, over every window, door and portal in the asylum.

BAM! BAM! BAM! BAM! BAM!

Every possible escape route had just been sealed off.

"No ..."

BAM!

The sound of the last iron plate landing in place echoed through the halls and left, in its wake, an eerie and resounding silence.

She turned back around, dumbstruck. But a movement in the looking glass caught her attention, instantly replacing her despair with a cold rush of dread.

In the mirror's reflection stood Alice, her singular, terrifying form only partially visible within the shadows that gave her strength. She raised a mottled arm and pointed in the direction of the basement door.

Nellie shook her head and stumbled backward.

Alice's yellow eyes gleamed in the shadows. "Yes, Nellie. Release me, and I will return Rose."

"Nellie!"

The sound of Dr. Braun's voice coming toward her pulled her attention from the mirror to the hall from which she had just come minutes before. The doctor ran toward her, his lab coat flying out behind him, just steps ahead of several orderlies.

"Stay away from me," she said, with an edge in her voice, her body tensed for attack.

"It's no use, Nellie. This whole place is on lockdown." Even as the words were spoken, the doctor cautiously put one foot in front of the other to close the distance between them.

She glanced into the mirror. Everything seemed to be back to normal.

She looked back to the doctor and the orderlies edging closer. They froze.

Nellie shook her head and waved her finger admonishingly, back and forth.

"There's nowhere to go." He took another step toward her.

She returned his gaze and tilted her head with a disapproving sigh. "That's what you think."

In an instant, she turned and bolted for the basement door.

CHAPTER 23

Nellie had no time to turn and gauge the distance to the men who were following fast on her heels. She leapt down the stairs, plunging pell-mell into the darkness of the corridor below. If there was a bright side to her predicament, it would be that her familiarity with this corridor was well beyond that of her pursuers, who she could hear tripping and clattering after her in the shadows.

Ahead, the light bulb at the end of the passage flickered. Contrary to each time she had previously witnessed it, this time its flickering filled her with hope.

"STOP!" Dr. Braun roared. The orderlies skidded to a halt around him, forming a wall that Nellie would not be able to pass. "It's over, Nellie. Come with us."

She grabbed the handle of the large wrench that kept the vault door sealed. "I'll open it!" she threatened.

Dr. Braun shrugged. "It doesn't matter. Alice died years ago."

"You really think death is enough to stop something like Alice?"

Dr. Braun felt the brunt of her disapproving expression and his face flushed with anger. He took a step toward her, fists curled at his sides.

Nellie jerked the wrench. Bolts inside the door clacked with movement. Dr. Braun's hand shot up, like a red flag, to signal that they cease their approach immediately.

She prepared to put her full weight on the wrench handle, but waited for a moment. She locked eyes with the doctor.

"You knew."

"Knew?" he repeated, the tone of his voice bordering on mocking.

"You knew I was pregnant. All along, you knew."

"Nellie! Listen to me," he blustered. "It's not what you think!"

"What is it then?"

"We just want you to get better. You're over reacting ... that's all."

"Then explain the baby! How is this possible?"

"We will find answers, Nellie. Things are not always what they seem. But if you would trust me ..." he held his hands out to her, imploring.

Nellie's grip on the wrench loosened. "Rose. The baby's name is Rose."

He smiled. "That's a beautiful name, Nellie. You need to get well for yourself, and for little Rose."

For just a moment, Dr. Braun and Nellie regarded one another with mutual understanding. Rose.

"Mommy?"

The sound of Rose's timid voice coming from somewhere inside Alice's room pulled Nellie instantly toward the vault door.

"Where are you, Mommy? It's dark in here. I can't see you …"

"I'm coming, baby," she whispered, and pulled the wrench handle the rest of the way down. Dirt pattered down from the ceiling as the great vault door disengaged from its seal.

"Stop!" Dr. Braun cried out in horror. "What are you — "

The walls and floor began to tremble. The orderlies looked to one another for explanation, and then glanced all around the foreign basement. They did not know whether to assist in subduing the runaway inmate or to run from the corridor posthaste.

The vault door swung open with a groan, and the tunnel filled with a blast of blinding white light that sent shock waves flowing through the corridor. The doctor, the orderlies, and Nellie cried out in pain as they were thrown to the ground.

And then … darkness.

CHAPTER 24

The door to the Saturation Chamber hung open on a single hinge. The orderly lay on the floor, dazed, while the hazy smoke that filled the room lingered in the air above him.

The Saturation Chamber was empty and silent as a tomb. Dorothy was gone.

The dark corridor was deathly quiet, the vault door now wide open. Dr. Braun, Nellie, and the orderlies lay scattered and stunned on the musty dirt floor.

One by one, the orderlies began to stir.

"What happened?" An orderly pulled himself up into sitting position and held his aching head. Dr. Braun followed suit first getting onto his hands and knees.

Nellie's fingers twitched. She moaned and let her head fall to the side, pain surging from the spot that had so recently impacted the tiled floor. Her eyelids fluttered as she struggled to open them. Her surroundings, albeit blurrily, started to reveal themselves.

Small, dirty bare feet stepped swiftly past her head.

Nellie forced herself upright as the orderlies' cries of terror filled the corridor. Dr. Braun ran, just ahead of them, toward the stairs at the end of the hall.

Her vision swam into focus in time to see the terror that staggered after them. Years of confinement had transformed the girl. Gray skin stretched over Alice's skeletal frame; bones bulged and jutted with each halting step.

"Alice ..." Nellie struggled to stand, her body's weakness having become nearly debilitating. She pulled herself up, and, using the wall for support, made her way to the stairs and up to the first floor.

Nellie found Alice amid the chaos, standing stock-still before the ornate looking glass. Nurses and orderlies alike screamed in terror and ran from the sight of the emaciated ghoul whose posture was distorted and whose limbs twisted with pain.

Nellie limped along the wall toward Alice as staff ran past her and unlocked doors to set the inmates loose. Those who had heard the stories knew that there would be little time to find a way out of Bedlam before history repeated itself.

A shrill sound like a diamond dragging across a glass surface filled the room. Nellie looked into the mirror and saw the cracks spreading. It was as if someone or something was pushing against the glass from the other side. Many Alices appeared in the broken shards, as the cracks multiplied.

A sinister black smoke rushed out of the cracks in the mirror and swarmed above the broken girl. It seemed to break apart into separate and unique vapors, and then in a rush, it enveloped Alice.

"What in God's name ..." Nellie whispered, mouth agape.

The black smoke swirled around Alice, and her whole body seemed to swell with energy. Nellie could now make out faces in the smoke as it circled and enshrouded the girl. Her demons had come through.

The Mad Hatter's unmistakable visage, with its glinting, red eyes, erupted from the cloud and gave Nellie a wicked grin.

"We're baaaaaaaaaacccccckkkk!" he announced, eyes flashing. The black smoke swirled about for another moment, before Alice breathed in deeply and wisps entered her through her eyes, mouth, and nose until the vapor had been completely absorbed. She closed her yellow eyes, hung her head, and swung around to face Nellie. Her matted hair hung in her face.

"I just want Rose back," Nellie said carefully. "You said you would give her back to me."

Alice opened her eyes. They shone white.

Nellie grabbed the wall for support.

Wordlessly, Alice turned and staggered up the stairs.

FWOOOOOOSHHHH!

With each step she took, flames roared up the walls on either side of Alice. The screams of torment from the souls on the second floor reached Nellie's ears.

"ALICE, STOP THIS!" she cried out, at the top of her lungs, pulling herself up the stair railing toward Alice's wake of destruction.

Orderlies turned on each other. Patients fell to the floor, howling and scratching their eyes out. Nellie reached the second floor to find an inmate who had successfully managed to pull her eyeball from its socket.

Alice continued down the hall, paying Nellie's pleas no heed.

Nellie struggled to reach her, ducking inmates and dodging the ever-rising flames.

"Alice! Alice!" came the pleas and wails of the inmates. "Please, Alice!"

Alice stopped in the green hall and turned to face

the door to a patient's room. She stretched out her fingers and touched the name that was stenciled there: DOROTHY GALE. Her fingertips pressed into the name, and the door began to smoke and smolder under her touch. Blackness crept outward from the spot until a flame leapt up and Dorothy's name was engulfed in fire.

With a wave of Alice's boney hand, Dorothy's door flew off its hinges and smashed against the far wall. Alice stepped into the doorway to find the room empty.

"Alice, don't do this," Nellie said.

Alice stared into the room and would not turn toward Nellie. She took another step cautiously toward Alice.

"Dorothy must be destroyed." The raspy voice filled Nellie's head.

"You are free now. There is no need for any of this violence."

"Don't you see, Nellie? We both need the same thing." Alice's shoulders and back rose and fell with great shuddering breaths. "Revenge." The word resonated throughout her body.

Nellie could feel the pain of more than a decade of torment wash through her. The little girl whose ability no one else could begin to understand — abused, forsaken, forgotten. She reached out to touch the girl's shoulder, but hesitated.

"Alice ..." she said softly.

Alice spun around, and Nellie jerked her hand quickly back. A blue light shone on them both. Nellie cautiously turned and then sharply inhaled.

Dorothy stood behind Nellie, her entire body radiating a dark, blue aura.

The flames on the walls had been extinguished, leaving them only smoldering. The victims of Alice's whims, who had fought against one another, who had crawled upon the floor, wailing in pain, all now lay quietly on the floor, asleep in the calming blue light of this girl.

Nellie stepped back from Alice. The black smoke came pouring from her to swirl and build behind her.

"Dorothy Gale of Kansas ..." the ghastly voice intoned.

Faces emerged from the billowing black cloud that continued to swell behind her like an ever-increasing shadow. The wisps and curls of its tendrils enveloped Alice's shoulders and arms as each demon's face emerged. Snapping claws, pointed teeth, glowing eyes — all were trained upon Nellie and Dorothy.

Then, out from the towering shadow, emerged a set of shiny blades, followed by an arm, followed by a top hat containing a caged brain. The Mad Hatter grinned maniacally and took his place next to Alice. The March Hare was the next to emerge. One by one, each of Alice's demons took their place behind Alice, whose eyes shone white like the center of molten rock.

"Dorothy, you had better do something," Nellie's voice cracked. The Cheshire Cat's wicked grin appeared — the shiny, metal, razor-sharp teeth materializing before the rest of its mangy, diseased body could cross through the portal of smoke and shadows.

"I can't do anything against demons!" Dorothy hissed, stepping backward as the Queen of Hearts emerged in her dress made of stitched human flesh held by chains and hooks. "This isn't Oz!"

The Cheshire Cat leaped over Alice to land with a heavy thud in front of them. It flashed its razor sharp talons and emitted a deep-throated growl that transformed into a hair-raising hiss. Its body lowered and tensed, ready to spring.

"Oh God ... RUN!" Nellie cried and grabbed Dorothy's wrist.

They broke into a sprint, the impact of each footfall firing blinding pain up through Nellie's calves. It felt like knives twisting between her muscles and bones.

The Cheshire Cat's backside wiggled playfully, as its crazy smile stretched from ear to ear. It pulled back and readied to pounce on the fleeing girls.

"Cheshire," Alice's papery voice interrupted.

It paused and turned patiently to its mistress, rolling its inky eyes.

"We'll get them later. Right now, we have other matters to attend to. He is closer to us now."

The enormous cat-demon growled menacingly in the direction of the prey that had been allowed to make its escape. It swung its massive head around and slunk into dark shadows after Alice and her army of horrors.

CHAPTER 25

F ind an outside line. Someone! Anyone!" Nurse Ball's voice wavered. "We need someone to reverse the lockdown from the outside!"

Nurse Murphy's fingers flew across the telephone switch board panel, pulling connections from ports and shoving plugs into open ports, each time listening for the click of an external line.

With all of his might, Dr. Braun used one hand to pull on the cage door of the operator's station while his other hand desperately twisted the key in the lock. The difficulty came chiefly from the three inmates who clung to the cage by their fingers and toes, screaming, "ALICE HAS COME! ALICE HAS COME!"

Nurse Ball pulled on the cage door along with the doctor, and the key engaged, allowing them to open the door.

"Belay that!" Dr. Braun strode to the operator's panel and yanked three of the cords from their receptacles. Nurse Murphy turned to protest, but Dr. Braun cut her short. "We cannot risk external contamination!"

And that was Nurse Ball's last straw. In the many years that Nurse Murphy had been in Nurse Ball's employ, she had seen countless scoldings and reprimands, the likes of which could make a drill sergeant weep. But never had she witnessed the head nurse lose control. Nurse Murphy's mouth fell open at the sight. The color in Nurse Ball's face resembled that of a beet, her eyes bulged, and the veins of her neck and temples throbbed.

She marched over to Dr. Braun, grabbed his lab coat and shirt in her fists, and nearly lifted the man's feet from the floor. "You!" she bellowed, all composure thrown to the wayside. "This is all *your* fault! You should NEVER have resurrected Project Alice! Your selfishness and incompetence has killed dozens of helpless patients and now endangers all of us. We are trapped in this godforsaken stone tomb with no way to get help. There are wildly insane THINGS wandering our halls killing without mercy or reason. Your crazed experiments and wild ideas will be the death of us all and for what?" She leaned into his face until she was nose to nose with the wide-eyed man.

He grabbed her hands and forcibly uncurled her fingers from his clothing. "You forget your place, nurse!" He put particular emphasis on the last word, and continued. "I make the calls here. After all, I am the doctor." He did not break contact with Nurse Ball's challenging stare as he tugged his attire back into place.

An eerie wail traveled down the halls of the dark asylum, becoming louder and louder, and then passing by, like a screech owl flying overhead in the dead of night.

The colors of rage rapidly drained from both Dr. Braun and Nurse Ball's faces as they turned to locate the source of the sound. Nurse Murphy stood, her forgotten headset clattering to the floor, eyes searching the ceilings and high walls.

There, on the ceiling at the end of the hall, black shadows flowed and curled like smoke toward them.

Dr. Braun breathed in, the horror setting in. Alice's demons ...

"Mother!" he whispered. Then he unlocked the cage door and bolted down the hall to the stairway.

Nurse Ball grabbed the swinging cage door and slammed it shut again, locking him out.

"Good riddance!" she spat.

Nellie and Dorothy ran down the hall toward the wailing that echoed down the corridor from the west wing, bringing them to a sudden stop. This was neither inmates nor staff. No mortal could make that sound.

WAAAAIIIIIIIIIIIIIIIIIIIIIIIIIIIIIIIIIIIIIIIIIIIIII ...

The unearthly keen flew from the west wing, over their heads, and down the corridor as if traveling at supersonic speed throughout the asylum.

Another blast zoomed past them from the wall, the sound so loud at its closest point that they ducked to the floor and held fast to one another.

Dorothy pointed, and Nellie saw movement from the inky shadows. A blood-curdling scream erupted from the patient's room just beyond the moving shadow.

"Dorothy! Dorothy! Listen to me. You need to stop this!" Nellie grasped her shoulders and stared into her tear-filled eyes.

"But ... I can't."

"Yes you can. The doctor said you have the same powers as Alice does."

"But she's summoning demons into this world! I've never done that before!"

"I think you have. Remember, on the boat ride? You told me that the scarecrow burned down your barn.

How did he get there? You must have brought him over somehow. Think."

Dorothy nodded. Closing her eyes, she tried to recall what she had been thinking in the barn when the scarecrow stood before her, arms raised. She remembered the dead, thin skin stretching over the face, the yellowed teeth, the way it grinned as if pleased by her fear. She trembled, straining to summon the blue aura that had sent the fifteen-foot monstrosity flying backward.

Nellie watched her carefully, searching every pore for any sign that Dorothy had succeeded in finding the trigger to her supernatural powers. But Dorothy's eyes popped open and she shook her head.

"Let's think. How does Alice bring her demons through?" Nellie sat back on her heels and counted out the facts on her fingertips. "She has to create a link from our world to Wonderland, through some sort of bridge, or portal, or —"

Chaos continued to erupt around them. The screeches and moans of the asylum's populace, inmates and staff, rent the air as the unearthly army of shadows brought devastation and agony.

Nellie suddenly grabbed Dorothy's arm. "I saw Alice by the mirror. She was pulling the demons through it. Maybe that's what we need to do! Let's go to the mirror!"

"No, no. When the scarecrow came, there was no mirror in the barn."

"You must use a different type of bridge. Was there anything else there? Try to remember."

"No, it's just a barn. There was hay, and feed, and … oh!"

"Oh?"

"The sow. The scarecrow threw the sow at my feet and … it was horrible. There was blood everywhere." Dorothy looked away.

"You created Oz from disaster and death," Nellie whispered, recalling the Mad Hatter's words. She turned Dorothy's face to hers. "Dorothy, I think your link to Oz is blood."

CHAPTER 26

D r. Braun arrived at the base of the last flight of stairs, gasping for breath, heart thumping, knees aching, and waves of pain rolling up his legs and lower back. His doughy body fought his every step upward, but he was now almost to the sixth floor, with its precious locked door at the end of the corridor.

He stood with his foot on the first step, panting, his lungs on fire. He pressed his hand into a sharp pain in his right side. The lights began to flicker. Dr. Braun gasped and looked all around him. One by one, the stairwell lights blinked out. Floor one — dark. Floor two — dark. Floor three — flicker ... dark. As the light diminished, the darkness crept up the stairs toward him.

There were voices now; he knew he was no longer alone. A distinct, high-pitched giggle and a deep-throated moan echoed up the stairwell from a floor below the step upon which he currently stood. It hissed, the HIIIISSSSSSSSSSSSSSS swirling and curling round the stairwell and up the steps that led to his position.

The shaking man fought the paralysis that swept through every inch of his body. Pushing through the pain of his frozen muscles, he turned and looked over his shoulder.

The fourth floor light went out. And, out of the darkness, two glowing red eyes emerged, followed by a maniacal cackling. The thing pulled itself up onto the next step in a spiderlike fashion, its elbows protruding to either side.

Dr. Braun whipped around and jumped up each step as fresh adrenaline pumped through his arteries. The light on the fifth floor landing went out behind him. The sounds got closer.

Dr. Braun leapt to the top step and threw open the door to the sixth floor, the piercing giggling just behind him. Something scraped across the heel of his shoe, injecting searing pain, as he dove across the threshold. He slammed the door shut, and twisted the deadbolt.

He glanced down to the back of his shoe to find the leather heel sliced open by two razor blades. A third razor had cut directly into the meat of his heel. The tendon could be severed. Blood oozed out onto the floor.

KA-BAM!

The door jumped in its frame with a sound like a shotgun blast. A frustrated, eerie screech reached a phenomenal pitch as the things on the other side of the door tried to burst their way through.

KA-BAM! BAM, BAM, BAM, BAM, BAM!

Dr. Braun hopped on his uninjured foot and bounced off the wall for support in order to make it to the end of the corridor. Blood dribbled in his wake, leaving a grisly trail in the flickering light.

The sounds of the door handle jiggling were soon drowned out by the jingling ring of keys as he unlocked the heavy door of patient White.

BOOM!

As Dr. Braun dragged his bad leg into the room and prepared to lock the door, the stairwell door blew open and the broken deadbolt clattered to the tile floor. He drew in ragged breaths and watched a giant, demonic cat head creep around the corner of the stairwell door, its black eyes rolling with delight. It sniffed at the pool of his blood on the landing and then lapped at it with its diseased, black tongue. The Mad Hatter crept out of the stairwell and stood fully upright next to the Cheshire Cat, who followed the blood trail to lick up every delicious drop. The Hatter's red, glowing eyes caught Dr. Braun peeking through the doorway. The fiend giggled, bowed low without breaking eye contact, and doffed his hat and brain. The tips of the shiny blades protruding from his sleeve glistened with the doctor's blood. Dr. Braun slammed the door shut and twisted the key in the lock.

There she lay on her white pillow, her blanket tucked in perfectly around her. Her chest rose and fell with shallow breaths; her hair lay neatly brushed and arranged on the pillow just as he had left it the night before.

He grabbed the chair, hopped with it to the locked door, and shoved it beneath the door handle. Feverishly he searched the room for anything he could find to jam under it. He found a towel, the nightstand, a pillow; he had lost all sense of reason.

"Mama," he cried, and grabbed her hand. He pulled the small hand mirror out of its drawer and grasped it tightly in his other, sweaty hand. "Please, mama! If you can hear me, please, oh God! Save me! She's coming for me!"

Red blood pooled around his shoe on the ebony black and pristine white tile.

He concentrated on the mirror, imagining the beautiful green forest, the blue birds, the thatched cottage. He gripped her hands so tightly that his shook, his skin turning yellow and then white.

A strange silence had fallen upon the sixth floor. Nothing happened.

Hot tears flowed freely now from the trembling man. The great and powerful Braun wept, his world finally at an end.

"She...she's coming, mama. I've made so many mistakes. She's coming for...For everything...for everything...I've done."

No response came. Mrs. Braun continued to breathe as peacefully as she always had, her eyes closed, her cheeks rosy.

From outside her door, Dr. Braun heard someone singing softly, off-key. The mirror fell from his hand and clattered to the floor.

I'll tell thee ev'rything I can;
There's little to relate.
I saw a selfish man,
Whose ego was so great.

"Who is this selfish man?" I said.
"And how is it you live?"
And his answer drilled right through my head
Like water through a sieve.

The chair slid out from under the doorknob and across the floor of its own accord. Dr. Braun watched the keyhole as the tumblers fell into place without the key. Tears welled up and splashed down his face, his shoulders shaking with silent sobs.

His treatments cruel they all did fail:
He left me in a daze,
And when he came to use the drill,
I set them all ablaze;

The door opened wide. There stood Alice, her head and arms hanging. Dr. Braun's pant legs grew warm and wet as his body reached the pinnacle of fright.

Then I shook him from side to side,
Until his face was blue;
"And now the time has come," I cried,
"To do the same to you!"

She pointed to the doctor, and the upset chair righted itself, spun around, and shot across the floor into the backs of his legs, forcing him to sit.

From behind Alice, the shadows stretched to loom above and around her. And out from the darkness stepped the Mad Hatter and the Queen of Hearts. The purring Cheshire Cat curled around the doorframe, having followed the trail of blood and consumed every drop in the hallway. Its impossibly long, black tongue licked up the rest of the red spatters in the room with one luxurious and disconcertingly long stroke.

"Off with his head!" Alice commanded.

The Mad Hatter cackled and approached the doctor, dragging his shiny blades along the wall and leaving perfect cuts in his wake.

At Alice's command, the Queen of Hearts

obediently brought her arms up before her. Out from the wounds in her flesh dress shot streams of chains with hooks; they wrapped around Dr. Braun, binding him to the chair. With a final clank, the hooks embedded themselves into his skin and pulled tight. He shrieked through shuddering tears.

"Step One." The Mad Hatter bowed, with a sweeping gesture, toward the Queen of Hearts. "Sensory Deprivation."

The queen lifted her arms toward the ceiling. Her chains instantly snaked from around the doctor's chair and torso to anchor to the ceiling and walls, lifting him from the chair to suspend him horizontally above the floor by his arms and legs.

"No, please!" he cried out, his voice breaking. "It was all for the good of humanity. Alice, you must understand why!"

"Sensory Deprivation begins. Turn out the lights," the Mad Hatter giggled.

"First you needed total quiet. I had to eliminate all outside input!"

The doctor's explanation ceased and became a blood-curdling scream as the Queen of Hearts used her two long, pointed fingernails to scoop out his eyes. Blood ran from the sides of his face. She dropped both eyeballs to the floor where the Cheshire Cat had taken up his post, waiting for new morsels to consume.

"Step Two — so very shocking. The Cognome Machine," the Mad Hatter continued. "Oh, do stop with the incessant screaming, sir. It's very unbecoming for someone of your station."

He stepped around behind the doctor and grabbed the chains that bound the doctor's arms.

"Let's turn you on!"

White arcs of electricity jumped from the smiling man's hands, down the chains, and over Dr. Braun. His body convulsed upward into a rigid arch. Slammed with electric current, his teeth locked together and foam bubbled out of his mouth.

"Oh there you go. I bet your mind is clear now." The Hatter grinned and released the chain.

Dr. Braun's body went limp and swung slightly to and fro. He did not answer, having gone into shock.

Cheshire, having consumed the eyeballs and washed the blood from its mangled fur, reached up to drag its black tongue across the doctor's dripping ankle wound. Its tongue felt like small shards of glass, and served to widen the cut. The blood flowed faster, and the searing pain snapped the blind doctor back to consciousness.

"ALICE!" he screamed. "LISTEN TO ME!"

Alice stepped up onto the doctor's torso and leant down, perched like a gargoyle on his chest. She studied his bloody face with her yellow eyes.

"The Cognome Machine ... the electricity ... you needed it to connect to your world ... to see it ... what is it ... Wonderland? And then, we — we could go to the —"

"Step Three. The Saturation Chamber," the raspy voice finished.

"To let you project your world to us! To let us see the images and — and to get in! Don't you see, Alice?

You have a gift! You created a world! And I created a way to share it with the world!"

She tilted her head, staring at him silently.

"If only you would have worked with me. With my machines, there would have been peace! All of the sick, all of the insane ... to see your Wonderland and be part of it, all together, bringing peace to the minds of the mad with only one thought!"

Alice touched the center of his forehead. "To control them. To rule them. Like the Queen."

"For God's sake, Alice! I wanted to open your mind and share it with everyone! It could have controlled them all, cured them ALL! It's how my mother helped me ... with her world!"

"Open your mind, doctor," the dead voice filled his head.

"NO!" he screamed, as her small index finger pushed through his forehead.

POP!

The doctor's exquisite pain peaked as blood jettisoned from his cranium in an impressive fountain that rained down to the floor below. The Cheshire Cat leapt to hastily lap at the delicious treat.

Alice stepped down from her slackened perch.

"Come," she said and walked to the door. The Queen of Hearts withdrew her chains into her dress, and the doctor's body fell to the floor with a solid whump.

ROOOwwwwwwwwwRRRRR?

The Cheshire Cat prowled behind the lifeless body of Henry Braun.

"Go ahead. But don't be late," Alice answered without turning around.

Alice left the room with the Mad Hatter and the Queen of Hearts. The demon cat opened its maw wide and began to swallow the doctor mouthful by mouthful, starting with the feet and working his way up with only the sound of crunching bones.

The door to the check-in room hung ajar amid the

pandemonium. Nellie and Dorothy rushed inside and slammed the door shut.

"Look for your name!" Nellie urged, holding the door handle, lest an inmate or nurse try to force entry.

Boxes flew across the floor as Dorothy slid them out of her way. "Found it!" Dorothy cried. She pulled the silver, blood stained slippers from the box and hugged them. "I thought I'd never see them again!" She placed them on the ground and stepped into them.

"You ready?"

Dorothy nodded.

Nurse Ball ran down the hallway with her long hair flying out behind her, her white cap having fallen off two floors back when the demonic White Rabbit first began its pursuit. She glanced over her shoulder to find the creature still bounding after her, its skipping hops playful in sharp contrast to her long-legged, panicked strides.

The body of an orderly in her path sent the head nurse sprawling to the ground. She slid to a stop and put her palms to the ground in preparation to push herself back up. Her fingertips, however, touched small, bare toes.

Nurse Ball looked up and shrieked, scrambling backward from the form of Alice, leering over her.

"Alice Liddell. What — what have you done?" she stuttered.

CRACK!

The White Rabbit caught up to its prey, and shoved its giant walking stick into the nurse's spine. It lifted Nurse Ball up off the floor. She slid further down the stick, which then passed through her back and stomach. Blood ran from her mouth.

The White Rabbit's face was surrounded by metal contraptions which began to click and whir, slowly peeling back its skin. There, inside its face, was the upside-down head of Dr. Braun, screaming out in agony.

She turned back around, unable to scream or move, waiting for death to take her pain. Yet, unexpectedly, she was set back down to the floor to the sound of hair-raising screeching. Nurse Ball struggled to turn around.

There stood an impossibly tall and gaunt creature in a floppy, black hat. It was Dorothy's scarecrow, and it now lifted the White Rabbit off the floor by the metal shears it wore in place of hands.

The rabbit thrashed around wildly, kicking, screaming, and flailing against the metal shears that held it, stuck and bleeding, to the scarecrow's arms. Nurse Ball knew this could mean only one thing. She dragged herself by the elbows across the floor to see beyond the clashing demons. There stood Dorothy, side by side with Nellie.

"You can't hurt anyone else, Alice," Dorothy said, clenching her fists.

Alice did not respond, but instead took a staggering step toward them. Dorothy's body tensed.

An arm suddenly snaked around Alice's legs and clung to her tenaciously, halting Alice in her tracks.

"RUN! Get out of Bedlam!" Nurse Ball bellowed, with all of her strength. Blood ran from her lips as she locked her arms, fighting with Alice for control.

"Come with us!" Nellie cried out.

"GO! I'm already dead!" The nurse coughed up blood and spat, still struggling to keep the girl immobile. Alice's eyes turned from ghastly yellow to glowing white. Nellie and Dorothy watched in horror as Nurse Ball started to sizzle, smoke, and then burst into flames.

Nellie tugged at Dorothy's arm. "Let's go!"

They tore down the hall, leaving the scarecrow to finish the fight with the rabbit.

When they finally reached the asylum entrance and slid to a stop, they found that it was still locked down. Worse yet, a gruesome barrier had been erected in front of the door: a wall, made up of contorted and disfigured bodies of nurses, dead orderlies, and wire had been hung, arranged, and stapled. Layers of dried blood cemented the mass together, a human mortar and brick wall.

Nellie dropped to her knees and wept.

"You were right," Dorothy's small voice cut through the silence. "We have to fight."

CRACK!

They looked to the ceiling from where the abrupt sound had just come. A crack split the ceiling, and thick, black, smoke-like shadows seeped through and fell toward them. The darkness spread through the room, swallowing the light and swirling toward Nellie and Dorothy.

CHAPTER 27

Nellie looked toward the stairs for an escape route, but the black smoke fell down each step from that direction as well.

"Nell, stay back. It's my turn now." Dorothy closed her eyes and held her arms out at her sides, clenching her fists just as she had done in the barn on that fateful night.

Nellie gasped and scooted backward behind Dorothy. A blue aura had begun to shine from around Dorothy's entire being. Her silver slippers sparkled in the blue light, and a dark red viscous liquid flowed out from the slippers and spread across the floor toward the shadows.

From the blood-like growing puddle, a metallic hand shot upward. It was followed by the arm, shoulders, head and torso of a tin man, whirring and clicking as he crawled up from the floor to stand next to Dorothy.

Nellie watched in amazement as a great, tawny paw with deadly talons emerged and the brawny form of a lion hoisted itself upward. A green hand with long red nails pushed upward and flexed. One by one, hands and heads appeared from the liquid that formed the gateway from which the horrors of Oz could emerge.

The shadows roiled down the steps and fell from the ceiling to gather before the crimson pool. From the shadows, Wonderland's demons stepped forth to crawl and slither toward Dorothy.

"It doesn't have to end this way. Why are you doing this, Alice?"

The decaying form of Alice Liddell staggered to the front of her warriors. "They took Wonderland away from me. Twisted and distorted it with their sadistic experiments. I need a new place to call home. I rather like Oz."

"No! Just because they've destroyed your dreams gives you no right to take mine." Dorothy's blue aura strengthened with defiance.

"Doesn't it?" Alice's mottled, crimson lips cracked into a wicked grin. She glanced around at her army. Grotesque and mutilated, they were still hers. "Kill them," she commanded, with a gravelly voice. "Kill them all!"

The room filled with deafening sound — roars, screeches, screams, and wails. The walls of the asylum rattled and the forces of Wonderland and Oz clashed.

A flurry of claws, metal, skin and fur blurred together as demons from both sides leapt upon one another. The tin man chunked forward to grasp at the Mad Hatter, but the stealthy man in black velvet and human leather easily side-stepped him and drove his long razors into the tin torso. He pulled the lengthy razors upward, slicing through the tin and causing the organs that had so carefully been packed into its chest cavity to spill out onto the floor.

The Wicked Witch drove her long red nails into the chest of the Queen of Hearts, and the Queen countered by sending her metal chains around and around the witch's neck, pulling her backward.

The lion emitted a cacophonous roar when the March Hare drove its silver knife into the small of the Lion's back and twisted. Next to them, the White Rabbit slammed its walking stick straight through the March Hare's foot.

Nellie watched Dorothy and Alice stand motionless in the midst of the fray. Each concentrated on their demons, pushing them forward against one another. Dorothy's blue aura now surpassed Nellie to light the room where Alice's blackness towered over and behind her.

"Mommy?" A child's voice rang through the din of the war, and only Nellie could hear it.

"Rose?" Nellie scrambled to her feet and looked all around. There, in the mirror. The small girl with brown curls stood in the mirror's reflection, surrounded by light.

"What have you done with her?" Nellie shouted at Alice.

Alice glared at Nellie; the raspy voice echoed in her head. "She's safe," it snapped. "Safer than she was with the doctor."

"Give her back to me! She's got nothing to do with this. She's innocent!"

"If you want your daughter back, Nellie, kill Dorothy." The yellow eyes turned from her back to the battle.

The asylum was falling apart at the seams. Walls crumbled, flames shot up from curtains toward the ceiling to be extinguished by cold blasts of wind, shelves toppled and smashed to the floor. Weapons slashed and cut through wooden structures, demons gnashed and snarled, grasped at one another, threw one another to the ground.

The Mad Hatter grabbed the tin man by the arm and swung the metal creature directly into a crumbling wall where the pipes burst and sprayed hot water onto a yowling Cheshire Cat.

Nellie looked to Dorothy, who in a trance-like state commanded her warriors. A long thick metal pipe clattered from inside the wall to the floor and rolled toward Nellie. This was her chance. Nellie grabbed the pipe and dashed toward the center of the fray.

"DO IT!" Alice's voice screamed in Nellie's head.

Fury flowed through Nellie as she charged toward the girl. All she could think about was her baby, her precious Rose, trapped in the mirror and beyond her reach. Nellie dodged the lion's swinging arm and ducked beneath the White Rabbit's whirling walking stick. She lifted the pipe over her shoulder and brought it around and down with all her strength. It connected solidly with its target.

"Give me back my baby!" Nellie screamed, as Alice flew backward, the pipe connecting to Alice's head with a solid clang.

Alice rose right back up to her feet, and a burning pain entered Nellie's head like a hot knife through her eye. Nellie screamed, fell to her knees, and grabbed at her eyes.

But the break in Alice's concentration was what was needed. Dorothy raised her arms and pushed forward, her blue light overtaking Alice's shadow. The denizens of Oz grew larger. The tin man righted himself, his gashes mended together in a flash of blue light. The lion's arms and legs doubled in size, his claws protruding. The Wicked Witch kicked a striped leg forward to impale the March Hare with the long, sharp heel of her shoe and push him backward toward the mirror. The scarecrow swept his long arms into the fray and grasped the Mad Hatter. He pitched the flailing man with red eyes toward the ornate looking glass.

One by one, the demons of Wonderland backed up against the mirror and dissolved into black smoke. The smoke drifted up and into the cracks in the mirror, pulled by an unseen force.

"No!" Alice cried, clenching her fists at her sides. The White Rabbit picked his mistress up, kicking and flailing, to carry her toward the mirror. "NO! NO! NO!"

she shrieked. He put his paw to the mirror and together, they disintegrated into wisps of black smoke, pulled into the cracks.

The pain in Nellie's head ceased and she dropped to the floor, panting.

The warriors of Oz began their retreat. They stepped backward to stop in the crimson pool. And just as they had come into the world, they retreated back to Oz. As they did, the pool receded backward to Dorothy's sparkling silver slippers.

Dorothy slipped her feet out of the slippers and ran to Nellie.

"Are you alright, Nell?"

Nellie shook her head and ran to the mirror, slapping its glass surface with her palm. "Rose!" she yelled.

Only Alice's laughter answered. "If you want your daughter, you're going to have to come get her."

The reflection in the mirror wavered with white light. A portal had emerged. Through its center, Nellie and Dorothy could see small Rose in the distance in

Wonderland. She lay upon a metal bed surrounded by glass, eyes closed.

"ROSE!" Nellie shouted again.

"She will remain in my world. Forever. In a deep sleep."

The image dissolved and only Nellie and Dorothy's pale panicked expressions reflected back.

"Come to her, Nellie, if you dare. Come save your little Sleeping Beauty."

Nellie reached out to touch the looking glass with trembling fingers. But Alice's last act of defiance struck; a shock like high-voltage electricity passed through Nellie's hand and sent her flying backward to the floor with a painful thud.

Dorothy ran to Nellie and wrapped the broken and sobbing woman in her arms.

CHAPTER 28

L ifeless bodies littered the asylum floor. Papers fluttered through the air on currents of heat, whipped to a frenzy by the chaos that filled the nearby hallways.

Nellie used her good hand, and all of her remaining strength, to pull her bruised and battered body slowly across the floor toward the once white coat of a recently former orderly of the madhouse. Every inch forward wracked her body with pain, but it had been sheer will that had brought her through this nightmare, and it would continue to push her through what was to come next.

Her hand shook as she guided it into the pocket of the orderly's coat and found the thing she sought: a pen. The ringing in her ears continued as she pulled herself upward into a sitting position to rest against the wall. Her hand trembled, sliding one of the dirty pages from the floor to her side. Through the terror and exhaustion, she put pen to paper:

It seems strange that through some miracle I find myself alive, and the first thing I do is to find a piece of paper and write. I am, after all, a reporter at heart.

The worlds the girls have called Oz and Wonderland clashed together on this day. They were not fantasy lands or figments of youthful imagination. They were real — and inhabited by demons. This war began even before Dorothy and Alice met. And was I lucky or cursed that I was there to witness it all? What I write sounds absurd to every sense of the human experience. But I've seen it, heard it, felt it in my very soul. I know it to be true. And I know now what I must do.

Dorothy ran back from the hallway. "There's no one left. It's just us."

Nellie nodded and pulled herself up onto her feet. Leaning against the wall, she staggered toward the mirror.

"You can't go." Dorothy's eyes filled with tears. "If you go, I can't protect you. I don't know how to get into Wonderland."

"I can't abandon her. I'm all she has left." Nellie pulled the paper from her pocket and held it out to Dorothy. "Go … use this. Tell the world what happened here."

"You promised you would get me out of here."

"I'm sorry, Dorothy … I have to go."

"You promised!" Dorothy cried, her lower lip trembling. Nellie opened her mouth to speak, but stopped. There was something in Dorothy's eyes now, something that hadn't been there before. It was familiar somehow, and it sent a small wave of fear rippling through her exhausted body.

Nellie closed her eyes. "You need to stay here where you'll be safe." She leaned over, kissed Dorothy on the cheek, and turned toward the mirror.

"TAKE ME WITH YOU!" Dorothy screamed, with all of her might, her body shaking.

Nellie did not turn back, nor did she speak. With her head hung, she stepped through the mirror. Instantly, the cracks healed. The looking glass was again just a looking glass.

Dorothy rushed to the mirror, but it was too late. She collapsed to the ground and wept.

With a high-pitched whirring, the lockdown panels sprang to life and lifted up away from the windows and doors. The asylum staff members who had not been on duty arrived at the entrance, ready to assist with the aftermath of the lockdown. But what they found sent some screaming from the door, one to vomit, and others to run for help.

It took hours to clear a path and wheel the bodies out of the facility to be laid side by side on the lawn for identification. Of note, they were never able to find Dr.

Henry Braun. He was presumed to have been a casualty of fire.

Only Dorothy remained. The staff found her in front of the large mirror, sobbing and unable to answer questions. They escorted her out onto the lawn into the sunshine and fresh air.

Dr. Braun's office was another casualty of fire. His research, specimens, photographs, books, files — all were reduced to ash, and irretrievable. All save for one peculiar item.

The orderlies' normally white uniforms were covered in black soot as they transported burnt remains and debris outside.

A red headed orderly pulled down the rag he had tied over his mouth and nose long enough to speak to his companion. "What in the living hell is this, Randal?" He pulled a soot-covered sheet off of one of Dr. Braun's machines.

The Cognome Machine remained completely intact, with only remnants of ash littering the normally shiny screen and tubes.

"Hypnotic Machine: For Mass Use" he read from the label inside its metal frame.

"Oh yeah, Doug told me about it," Randal laughed. "Apparently he called it a," he held his fingers in the air indicating quotes, "'A Tele-Vision'. He said in the future everyone would have one in their house. It shows moving pictures, I guess, like at the theater."

"Oh! Just smaller and in your house? That sure would be the bees knees! But you'd hafta play your own piano music, I guess?"

"It's just a bunch of junk. Nurse Ball said so."

They both shrugged and wheeled the Tele-Vision out to the entrance on the way to the courtyard.

Dorothy stood in the doorway and smiled.

"'Scuse us, Miss," Chris nodded to her. "You gotta go back outside now."

Dorothy shook her head and stepped inside, shutting the door. The orderlies looked at each other. "Look, we don't want to get rough with you. C'mon, just listen, for once."

Dorothy stood before them with her arms taut at her sides and her fists clenched. She closed her eyes.

A wind surged around their feet, whipping and circling around the orderlies and sending papers flying and spinning about them.

"What the hell?" Randal said lifting his arms as the gale rose up his torso. Dorothy's aura began to emanate from all around. But this time, the gentle and calming dark blue was gone. This time, it was black. Like Alice's.

The orderlies dropped to their knees, screaming. Chris banged his head against the floor holding his ears while Randal pressed on his eyes.

And just as suddenly as it had begun, the pain stopped. Chris collapsed to the ground. Randal sat up and tried to see the door through his blurred vision. But the door was long gone. He rubbed his eyes and fell back.

EPILOGUE

It was nighttime, and they were outside on a brick path, under red skies filled with black storm clouds.

"What in God's name??" Chris cried, scrabbling up to his hands and knees. They were stationed at the bottom of a pedestal, upon which Dorothy reposed on a throne. Gone was the beautiful girl with rosy cheeks and perfect brown braids. In her place sat a female adorned by human skin and rubber-looking material stretched over her body. She was, in effect, wearing a macabre second skin. The throne was of metal, barbed wire, and chains with hooks that held her in place and tore at her flesh.

Dorothy leaned forward, pulling against the hooks and further stretching her gaping, pink wounds. "I'm your only god, here." She kicked one leg over the arm of the throne and leaned back. "Nellie said my powers are fueled by blood. I have to save her. I'm going after her."

Chris sprang to his feet to dart toward the tall black grass, but chains with hooks shot from the throne and latched into his shoulder blades. He cried out and collapsed to the ground.

Unfazed, Dorothy pointed to air above them. They followed her finger to the object suspended above them by chains: the ornate mirror from the asylum entryway. It radiated a powerful, black aura.

"But to go after Nell, I'll need an army ..."

Randal followed her blank stare down the brick path to the bottom of the hill. There, stood thousands upon thousands of snarling, snapping demons. Looking at them as they stood, line by line in formation, he could not see a beginning or an end.

" ...and *lots* of blood," she finished, leaning back down toward them.

Chris stammered, hanging on to the chains that dug into his back. "Wha — what? Who — who are you?"

Dorothy stood, towering over them. She crossed her arms and looked out upon her armies. "I am Dorothy Gale, from Kansas. And you will be my sacrifice."

Their queen raised her arms over her head and shouted, her voice echoing over their masses. The black shadow rose up behind and all around her throne.

The orderlies' screams of anguish and terror were instantly drowned out by the thunderous roars and cheers from below.

"Wonderland will regret the day they ever crossed us, the armies of OZ!"

TO BE
CONTINUED

BEDLAM STORIES

THE FALL OF OZ

THE UNIVERSE OF BEDLAM STORIES CONTINUES

Log on to our website

www.bedlamstories.com

Find out more

Project: Alice
The Lost Files

Step into the minds of Doctor Braun as he chronicles his full research of the doomed Project: Alice. Available as a free e-book in our member's area.

THE MISSING CHAPTERS

Read the missing Chapters of Bedlam Stories, available to all our members

SUBSCRIBE ONLINE FOR FREE ACCESS

Also hear the sound track

Read the original Alice in Wonderland and Dorothy of Oz books

Exclusive Merchandising

and more...

THE VAULT AWAITS

AUTHOR

Christine Converse has been a freelance writer since 1994.
Publishing credits include dozens of magazine articles, video game
strategy guides and books.

For the next several years, she wrote magazine articles for top
gaming magazines and published multiple guide books for games
about very popular plumbers, zombie apocalypses, vampires with
swords, aliens, replicants, jedi and more.

CREATOR

Pearry Teo is a film director who has worked on such films as Necromentia, Dracula: the Dark Prince and The Gene Generation. He is well known for his dark aesthetics and visuals in his work.

Pearry first envisioned Bedlam Stories in 2009 and created a visual compendium as a reference. In 2011, Together with Nicole Jones and Chad Michael Ward, they created the genesis of the script and laid out the foundation of what became Bedlam Stories.

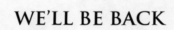
WE'LL BE BACK